BYRON'S CHILD

Also by Carola Dunn

BYRON'S CHILD

Carola Dunn

Walker and Company
New York

First published in the United States of America in 1991 by
Walker Publishing Company, Inc.
Published simultaneously in Canada by Thomas Allen & Son
Canada, Limited, Markham, Ontario

Library of Congress Cataloging-in-Publication Data

Dunn, Carola
Byron's child : Carola Dunn

ISBN 0-8027-1132-4
I. Title.
PR6054.U537B9   1991
823'.914—dc20   90-43706
CIP

Printed in the United States of America
2   4   6   8   10   9   7   5   3   1

"Nonsense, Emily. I am doing this for your own good." Roland's slightly plump cheeks quivered with annoyance. He was unused to rebellion, especially when his authority as head of the family was enhanced by the solemn dignity of his seat behind the desk in his library. "A green girl cannot possibly be expected to know what will be best for her."

"But he frightens me." Emily's soft brown eyes filled with tears. She blinked them back. Weeping always irritated her brother.

"You scarcely know the man. You cannot judge his character after standing up with him a couple of times at balls. You are excessively fortunate to have caught the earl's eye."

"I do not feel in the least fortunate. He has a horridly cutting tongue."

Having suffered himself, Roland looked a little conscious. "Naturally he will curb his sarcasm when you are betrothed."

"And when we are married?"

Unable to answer, he resorted to bluster. "Pray don't be pert, Emily. It is a splendid match. I leave in the morning to arrange the settlements and I shall bring him home with me the next day. There is nothing more to be said." He began to fuss with the papers on his desk.

Emily fled from the room, then stumbled to a halt in the passage outside. It was no use going up to her chamber. Charlotte would follow her there, and though her sister-in-law would sympathize she was also bound to counsel obedience.

1

The passage led to the back door out to the stables. At this time in the evening the grooms were doubtless in the kitchen eating their dinner. The horses would not prate to her of her duty to obey her brother.

Heedless of a distant rumble of thunder, Emily scurried across the stable yard. A lighted lantern hanging from a nail showed an empty stall, surely a safe refuge. Dropping to her knees on a pile of fragrant hay, she scarcely noticed how it pricked through the warm green wool of her gown. She hid her face in her hands and wept.

How could Roland be so brutal as to force her to marry a man who was a friend of the sinister Lord Byron?

== 1 ==

A BELL JANGLED as Jodie stepped into the dingy little shop. She glanced around at the shelves piled with dusty cardboard boxes. Radio Shack it was not.

Behind the scratched wooden counter a pimpled youth looked up from the soccer page of the *Oxford Mail*. "Yer?"

"I need a transformer so I can run an American hairdryer on English volts. Or is it amps? I can't do without it in this climate." She pushed back a clinging strand of straight black hair, damp from the drizzle outside.

"The boss is busy wiv Lord Faringdale's stuff right now." His attention already returning to his newspaper, the clerk jerked a thumb at a tall man in grey sweats who leaned against another counter, scribbling numbers in a catalogue.

Lord Faringdale? A real live lord? Despite her republican upbringing, Jodie regarded him with interest.

He must have heard her request, for he looked up. "Unless you need a transformer for other high-wattage appliances too, it'd be much cheaper to buy a new hairdryer, you know." His voice was a pleasant baritone, his speech precise in the educated English manner yet without affectation.

He looked thirtyish: fair hair, thick and wavy; features too irregular to be called handsome; eyes the colour of California skies. His grey outfit (a lord in a tracksuit!) revealed the long-legged, athletic build of a runner or basketball player.

Under her scrutiny he flushed slightly. Jodie realized she had not responded to his advice.

3

"Sh—darn! I could have bought a new hairdryer downtown instead of dragging all the way out here. I have digs in Headington," she explained, pleased with the anglicism, then glanced at the clock on the wall, grimacing, "and I've missed my bus. Not the first time. I've learned to take a book with me wherever I go." She patted her tote bag.

"Headington?" He hesitated. "I'm going that way. Would you like a lift?"

"Thanks, but I . . ." Jodie reconsidered. This was England, not America, and who could be more respectable than an English lord? "Thanks, that'll be great. I'm Jodie Zaleski."

"Giles Faringdale." His smile was crooked, unexpectedly charming. "I'm nearly done here. We'll take the ring-road and be there in no time."

When they set off a few minutes later Jodie was slightly disappointed to find he drove a Range Rover; she had hoped for a Rolls or a Bentley.

"I did hear right, didn't I?" she asked. "You're a lord?"

He looked embarrassed. "Yes, a viscount."

"Do I call you 'my lord'?"

"Please, call me Giles. I try to avoid the 'my lord' business."

"That's a very English name."

"It has alternated with Roland in my family for generations."

"Then I'm glad I hit the Giles generation. Thanks for the ride, Giles. It's a real hassle not having a car. My dad said he'd buy me one, but the traffic in Oxford scares me half to death. At least they drive on the right side of the road in La Jolla."

"You're from California? Jeans and high-heeled boots suit the image, but I thought all Californian girls were blondes."

She laughed. "That's a myth propagated by the tourist bureaus. My mom's half Chinese, though you can't tell by my eyes. I inherited the straight black hair from her. She's a biologist and she explained it all to me once."

"Are you a student here?"

"A Rhodes scholar," Jodie announced with pride. "I'm collecting material for the thesis I want to write when I get back home. It'll be a comparison of English city and country life in the early nineteenth century, so it's a real help to be over

4

here. Just being able to visit the old buildings makes it all seem real, though I haven't been to any stately homes yet."

She closed her eyes and gripped the seat as Giles drove the wrong way, in her view, round a busy roundabout, turning onto the Oxford by-pass. The next roundabout they would come to was in Headington. Would he ask for her phone number when he dropped her off—or did she dare ask for his? She didn't want to be thought a brash American, yet it seemed a pity to let a lord get away without making an effort. A real, live English viscount! She pinched herself.

"I wonder," he said diffidently, "whether you'd like to see my home. Waterstock Manor isn't really big enough to be called a stately home, but the house is little altered since Queen Anne's time. It's near Thame, about ten miles. If you have nothing better to do you could come now and I'll run you home later on."

"Hey, that sounds great!"

"I hope you won't be disappointed. We only have a couple of rooms furnished in period style. My mother believes in comfort before elegance."

"I guess you have plumbing and electricity then." Jodie grinned. "I was afraid to ask."

It had stopped raining, and the sun came out as they left the city behind. Ploughed farmland lay in long, gentle slopes on both sides; copses and spinneys glowed in autumn russet and gold. Hazy with distance, the wooded ridge of the Chilterns marched across the southeastern horizon.

"This is about as different as you can get from San Diego County," Jodie remarked. "I bet it hasn't changed much in a couple of centuries. What crops do you grow?"

"Barley, wheat, turnips, I think, and could it be beans? Sorry, I'm not much help. I'm a physicist, not a farmer."

"A physicist! You're kidding! As in quarks and cosmic strings and that? I figured you for a gentleman of leisure. You're a professor?"

"I'm not attached to the university; I work at home—and don't you dare say anything about mad scientists."

She laughed. "Okay. You must be purely theoretical, then?"

"No, I have a lab. It's rather an odd set-up, actually." Giles sounded embarrassed. "I won't go into details, but it suits me very well because I have a ridiculously old-fashioned attachment to my family's land."

Having moved five times in her life, Jodie thought ridiculous summed it up, but she tactfully did not say so. "What are you working on, or is it hush-hush?"

"A rather obscure problem connected with electron orbits and tunneling electrons. Do you want to know more?" He grinned as she wrinkled her nose.

"No, but I'd like to see your lab."

"Nearly there."

Ahead, Jodie caught a glimpse of a square, red brick house, half–hidden by trees. Moments later they turned into a courtyard surrounded by low brick buildings. A garage door opened automatically and Giles drove in.

"This is one end of the stables. Most of the rest is taken up by the lab, but I have a couple of riding horses at the far end. I'll introduce you to them, if you like, but first I must tell Mother there will be one extra for tea."

She followed him across the stone-flagged courtyard and into the house by a back door. "I don't want to be any trouble."

"She'll be happy to see you. There are plenty of people here during the week but the two of us rattle around a bit at the weekend, unless my sisters bring their families over."

"I'm not dressed for afternoon tea with a ladyship."

"Nor am I. Don't worry; since the sun came out, her ladyship will probably be in her gardening clothes." Giles led Jodie across a marble-floored entrance hall, and out through an exterior door onto a flight of steps. "Yes, there she is." He waved to a figure in the garden below and called, "Mother, I've brought a friend for tea."

A woman in shapeless tweeds and a blue headscarf set down her wheelbarrow and waved at them. "Very nice, dear. I'll just finish manuring the roses."

It was not at all what Jodie had expected of a viscountess, but nothing loath she returned the casual wave.

"No hurry," Giles assured his mother. "We'll do the grand

tour and meet you in an hour or so."

From the entrance hall they went up a wide marble staircase to a suite of light, airy, high-ceilinged rooms on the first floor, furnished in a variety of eighteenth-century styles. It reminded Jodie of a good antique store back home, though she was too polite to say so. Then she noticed two costumes arranged on dummies: a magnificent Georgian court dress, hooped and laced, and a high-waisted Regency gown of fine, dark-green wool trimmed with bows of apricot ribbon.

"Now this is interesting." Jodie inspected the Regency gown closely. "Most of the costume pictures you see are from fashion plates but this looks like it was an everyday dress. The jumper style is particularly practical because you can wear a blouse or a sweater under it, depending on the weather. Am I boring you?"

"Only a little." Giles grinned. "I'll tell you what, how about trying it on? It looks about your size. My mother would be thrilled to death to see you in it."

"It's in very good condition." She fingered the fabric dubiously. "I'd hate to damage it though."

"Try it on. You were saying you weren't properly dressed for tea with the viscountess."

"Okay, I'll do it, if you promise I won't be hanged, drawn, and quartered if I spill tea on it. I'll change behind that Chinese screen."

Carefully they undressed the dummy. Under the gown it was wearing a long-sleeved white blouse, frilled at neck and cuffs, and nothing else but a linen shift. Stays had been out of fashion for most of the Regency period, Jodie remembered, just making a comeback toward the end, though probably old-fashioned women, and those more generously endowed, had never given up some sort of support.

"I'd better keep my own underwear on underneath," she said, taking the garments round behind the dragon-painted screen. She stripped off her jeans and sweater and put on the shift. As she donned the blouse, she realized it buttoned behind. "Giles, will you do it up for me, please? It seems to fit pretty well."

His fingers dealt deftly with the tiny buttons, sending a shiver down her spine. She cast an oblique glance over her shoulder. His face was serious, concentrating on the task. Nonetheless, though she had frequently appeared on the San Diego beaches in the skimpiest of swimwear, she wondered whether she had been wise to invite such intimate contact.

She trusted Giles, recently though she'd met him. It was herself she was not sure of. He was an attractive man, and she had broken up with Brad six months ago, when she told him she was going to England. It would be crazy to get involved in a futureless relationship with an English lord.

"There you are." He finished the buttons. "Can you manage the dress?"

"I think so."

He retreated. She slipped the gown over her head, tying the long ribbons in a bow beneath her breasts, and emerged into the room to examine herself in an ornately framed cheval glass.

"Hey, that's not bad. My hair's all wrong but the boots don't look as out of place as I expected." She turned and performed an approximation of a curtsy.

"Very elegant." He laughed. "I won't attempt a bow. Let's go down to the lab before tea."

"You're sure your mom isn't going to mind me wearing this?"

"It will amuse her," he promised.

Unused to long skirts, Jodie stumbled on the stairs. At once Giles reached out to steady her. "Careful. Mother won't be amused if you break your neck."

"Thank heaven for pants," Jodie exclaimed. "Dressing this way all the time would be a real pain in the you-know-what."

They crossed the courtyard again and Giles unlocked a door into the central part of the stable block. The long room inside was flooded with sunlight from west-facing windows. Polished metal gleamed, and the level hum of well-behaved machinery filled the air. Jodie recognized nothing but a row of blank computer screens.

"There's nothing much to see," Giles apologized. "The accelerator is running and the computers are crunching numbers." He turned on a screen, hit a few keys, and a moving graph glowed blue on silver.

"Just like a hospital scene on TV."

"On Monday, when my staff come in, it'll be all ready for us to have a go at guessing what it means. Wait a minute, that's odd." His fingers danced over the keyboard; the graph moved backwards and stopped. "I'd better check," he muttered, and strode over to the impressive, instrument-laden bulk of the accelerator.

Jodie followed him. He peered at a set of dials. Leaning closer to see what he was looking at, she brushed against his shoulder.

The world shuddered and went black.

= 2 =

HER EARS RINGING from the boom of the explosion, Jodie cautiously raised her head from Giles's chest. In the pitch darkness, she had no intention of leaving his remarkably comforting embrace.

"Wow," she said weakly. "I've heard of an electrifying relationship but . . ."

A brilliant flash of white light dazzled her, followed at once by a crack of thunder. The after-image left on her eyes made no sense.

Giles's arms tightened around her. "Stables." He sniffed. "Horses. What the hell?"

Another sheet of lightning. A pause before the thunderclap, which rattled and rumbled its way to uneasy silence. In the silence, the sound of hiccuping sobs.

"Someone's crying," Jodie muttered in Giles's ear. As her vision adjusted, she noticed a pale glimmer to her left, cut off by a shoulder-high partition. She pulled away from Giles and tiptoed towards the light, feeling ahead for obstacles.

"Jodie, come back," he whispered. "Jodie!" Shuffling sounds suggested that he was coming after her.

An old-fashioned lantern hung from a nail, illuminating a circle of straw-bestrewn flagstones. In the dimness beyond the circle, a weeping girl huddled on a pile of hay.

Something touched Jodie's back. She froze.

Giles, of course. "Don't do that," she said crossly.

The girl sat up and stared at them, a look of terror on her tear-blotched face. Staring back, not much less terrified, Jodie reached behind her for Giles's hand and clutched it.

The girl was wearing a green dress with pale orange ribbons, identical to Jodie's.

Even as she realized the similarity, the fabric of her historic gown disintegrated about her, turning to dust, leaving her standing there in bra, pantyhose and boots, with her tote bag slung over her shoulder.

A large, equine head appeared over the nearest partition and neighed disapprovingly. Jodie nearly jumped out of her skin. She flung herself back into Giles's arms, the only sane place in this madhouse. At least, that was what she intended. Since he was quick-wittedly whipping off his sweatshirt to cover her near-nakedness, she merely succeeded in making him stagger backwards, while she lost her balance and sat down.

"What the bloody hell?" came his muffled protest from behind her.

Scarcely daring to take her eyes off the girl, who now looked more shocked than frightened, Jodie glanced back. Giles was groping blindly for the hem of his sweatshirt, hopelessly entangled. She scrambled to extricate him. Freed from the garment's pythonic coils, he pulled it over Jodie's head, inside out, and she slipped her arms into the sleeves. With one accord they turned back to the girl.

She was gaping in apparent fascination at Jodie's legs, nylon-clad below the thigh-length sweatshirt. Her gaze switched to Giles's lean but muscular torso, revealed by his white tank top. Flushing, she closed her eyes and buried her face in her hands.

"Don't cry." Jodie hurried forward. "What's the matter?"

The girl jumped up and backed away until she was stopped by the stable wall.

"What's going on?" Giles chimed in. "What happened to my lab? Who are you?"

"Emily Faringdale," she squeaked. When they came no closer she gathered her courage, cleared her throat, and asked, "Who are you? And what are you doing in my brother's stables?"

"Faringdale? Your brother?" Giles looked stunned.

"I'm Jodie Zaleski and this is Giles. . . ." Jodie's voice

trailed away. "Emily Faringdale? What's your brother's name?"

"Roland, Viscount Faringdale. And he is the greatest beast in nature," she said vehemently, her grievances overcoming her fear.

"What's he done? Is that why you were crying?" Jodie, too, was distracted from the extraordinary situation.

"He says I must marry Lord Thorncrest. Lord Thorncrest is a friend of Byron," she added, as if that explained everything.

"Byron the poet?" Jodie clasped her bag, which contained the biography of Lord Byron's daughter she had bought that morning. "George Gordon, Baron Byron? Who wrote *Childe Harold*?"

Emily nodded, puzzled.

"A *friend*?"

"Ye gods," said Giles, "we've travelled through time."

"You can't be serious," Jodie said uncertainly. "That only happens in science fiction."

"How else can you explain this?" His gesture embraced the dimly lit stables, Emily's uncomprehending face, the smell of horses and the sound of their shifting feet. "Five minutes ago we were in a sunny laboratory. What's the date?" he asked Emily.

"The twentieth of February."

"Year?"

Her eyes widened in alarm. "1816."

"You see?" Turning to Jodie, who could think of nothing whatever to say, he put his hand to his chest and frowned. "Damnation, I haven't got my calculator."

"Your calculator!" Jodie felt the beginnings of hysteria. "Here I am stuck in the past with no clothes and all you can worry about is your damned calculator!" She shivered.

"If I can work out what brought us here, perhaps I can reverse the effect," he pointed out reasonably. "I'll have to make do with pencil and paper. Can you provide pencil and paper, Miss Faringdale? And something for Jodie to wear, so I can have my pullover back?"

Reminded of their indecent condition, Emily blushed

again. Her timid answer was drowned by a renewed rumbling of thunder and the rushing hiss of a sudden downpour.

"I wonder if it was something to do with the lightning," Giles muttered.

"Please help," begged Jodie, her teeth chattering.

Emily picked up a shawl she had dropped unnoticed in the straw, and handed it to Jodie. "I do not know who you are, and I cannot understand half the words you use, but I will try to help you," she said bravely. "Only I daresay Roland will be very angry if I take you over to the house. If we could wait until he leaves tomorrow . . . but you cannot spend the night here."

"He's leaving tomorrow?"

"For two days, to arrange the marriage settlements. Then he will bring Lord Thorncrest back for the formal betrothal." Emily dashed away a tear.

"You shouldn't let your brother dictate to you." Jodie's feminist blood was rousing. "Sneak us into the house tonight, and I'll deal with him when he comes back. He sounds like a regular tyrant."

Giles grinned. "Be careful what you say about my great-to-the-nth-power grandfather." Both girls stared at him and he shrugged. "Since the title always passed in the direct line, that, after all, is what Roland Faringdale must be."

Wearing his $great^n$-grandfather's nightshirt, Giles lay on his back, hands behind his head, staring at the sliver of moonlight on the ceiling. His mind racing with speculation, he was almost unaware of the discomfort of the sheetless, too-short bed, the musty chill of the nurse's room.

A floorboard creaked. He turned his head as the door to the night nursery opened. A ghostly figure appeared: Jodie, in his $Great^{n+1}$-Aunt Emily's all-enveloping nightdress.

He raised himself on one elbow. "What's wrong?"

"Nothing. I'm cold and I can't sleep." Her voice was small and frightened. "Can I get in with you?"

Giles moved over to make room. She spread the quilt from her own bed over him, then slipped in beside him.

Catching the glint of a tear on her cheek, he put his arm around her with a silent vow that the gesture was purely for comfort.

She snuggled against him. "Talk to me. Tell me about your lab, how you set it up at Waterstock Manor, what you do there, how it got us into this mess. Where did you go to school?"

"Cambridge, with some post-grad work in America and Germany." Despite his good intentions, Giles could not prevent his body's reaction to her closeness. He rolled over on his back again and forced himself to concentrate on his story. "I had quite a few job offers, but as I told you, I didn't want to leave my home."

"I don't blame you. I might have thought it ridiculous before, but after coming back a couple of centuries and finding your ancestors right here in the same place—well, it makes sense." Jodie sounded interested, more relaxed. "So you decided to set up your own lab. Doesn't that stuff cost millions?"

"I'm rather well-off," he said apologetically. "Of course, I couldn't have afforded it on my own. I found a small college in America that had been given a huge endowment strictly for buying research equipment, though they had no buildings to house it. I was happy to provide suitable buildings, and for tax reasons I offered to work for nothing."

"I bet they jumped at it. You said that was an accelerator we were standing by? I thought they were miles long."

"Some of them are. Mine just spits out electrons. Have you heard of tunneling?"

"Only the kind they're doing under the English Channel."

"I don't want to get too technical, but it's a phenomenon where electrons disappear on one side of a barrier and reappear on the other. We're trying to find out just where they go in between. A colleague of mine, an American woman at a lab near London, came up with a theory that they travel through time. I didn't take it very seriously, though the maths looked good, but it seems she may be right."

"It does, doesn't it? So your electrons decided to take a

hop to 1816 and brought us with them?"

"Something like that. I'm sure the lightning had something to do with it. It packs a hell of a high voltage. If only I had my calculator!"

"It's going to take a long time figuring it out by hand, isn't it?" said Jodie flatly. "We'll be here for a while, then. What about paradoxes? What if we change things so that the world we go back to, if we do, is different?"

Giles frowned at the ceiling. "I don't think there's much danger, if we're careful. Dr. Brown, the woman I told you about, had some law she called the Conservation of Reality. She claimed that any changes will tend to die away, like ripples on a pond. I think it only works for small deviations, but we should be okay as long as we don't do something drastic. Killing Roland, for instance, would surely be a paradox no mathematical law could deal with."

"I guess that would make you pop out of existence, like my dress did. I wouldn't want that to happen. Apart from you being my ticket home, I kind of like you." With those words Jodie turned her back to him, fortunately for his resolution. "I think I can sleep now. Good night, Giles."

"Good night, Jodie," he answered softly.

He lay for some time, staring into the darkness, thinking about the pretty, plucky girl at his side. Not by so much as a hint had she blamed him for their predicament. Nonetheless, he was responsible for her, and he would get her home if it was humanly possible.

As her breathing slowed in sleep, his mind once again filled with theories and numbers. If only he had his calculator!

When Jodie woke the next day, Giles was already up. The world seemed brighter in the morning, just as Mom had always told her. After all, she had been given a chance any historian would die for: to see her own period in person.

Eager to begin, Jodie hopped out of bed and went into the day nursery. In daylight the room was shabby, dusty, doubtless waiting to be refurbished for the next generation of Faringdales. Giles, dressed in his tracksuit, was at the battered table, scrawling his calculations on the paper

Emily had brought last night. He seemed to have mastered the quill pen.

"Good morning, my lord." There was no response. "Giles, I said good morning!"

He looked up in surprise. "Sorry. I get a bit wrapped up in my numbers. Good morning. You sound pretty chipper today."

"It finally sank in what a fantastic opportunity this is for research. How long can we stay?"

Emily had not provided slippers. The wood floor chilled Jodie's bare feet. Forgetting her nightgown's floor-length skirts she pattered towards the table to sit down. She caught her foot in the hem and stumbled into Giles's lap.

At that moment Emily opened the door and stared at them in shock. Daylight revealed her as a slim, pretty girl of nineteen or thereabouts, with medium-brown hair in ringlets and large, soft brown eyes. Beside her was a shorter, slightly plump girl, a year or two older, with fair, curly hair and a look of even greater shock in her blue eyes.

"Oh!" said Emily, and turned scarlet. "Oh dear."

Jodie felt her cheeks reddening, as if in sympathy. "I tripped," she explained, wriggling out of Giles's arms. "I'm not used to long dresses. At home I mostly wear pants or shorts."

"Pants?" Emily retreated a step as Giles politely stood.

"Trousers. Breeches." Jodie turned to Emily's dismayed companion. "Sorry about that. You must be Lady Faringdale. Hi, I'm Jodie Zaleski and this is . . . Emily told you?"

"Giles Faringdale?" she said hesitantly. "There is a family resemblance. But I cannot believe that you came from the future! Emily must have misunderstood."

"Indeed I did not. It is no stranger than Voltaire's tale of *Micromégas*, the traveller from Sirius. You remember, Charlotte, we read it together."

"Emily!" Her sister-in-law sounded appalled.

"They will not tell Roland that we have read Voltaire."

"Of course not," Jodie assured her. "But why not?"

"Because Voltaire was a freethinker. My brother would be excessively displeased."

"You mean the infamous Roland censors your reading?"

"He tries." There was a flash of mischief in Charlotte's blue eyes, though she continued with dignity, "However, he is my husband. Pray do not speak ill of him to me."

Jodie warmed to her. "Okay. I'm sorry."

Giles looked at the baffled faces of the young ladies and he laughed. "She means all right. Okay is an American expression, though by our time it's spread all over the world."

For the first time, young Lady Faringdale smiled, her round cheeks dimpling. "American! Of course, that explains a great deal," she said, then sobered. "I do not wish to seem inhospitable, but how long do you expect to be here? Roland is only away until midday tomorrow."

"Not a hope," said Giles flatly. "Even with a slide rule, it'll take longer than that, if they've even been invented. I'll have to go into Oxford and see if I can find one."

"Hey, great." Jodie was enthusiastic. "I can't wait to see Oxford in 1816."

"You'd better stay here. The less we wander around the less chance there is that we'll mess up the time stream irreparably."

"Giles Faringdale, if you think you can keep me cooped up in this place while you jaunt about the countryside, you've got another thing coming. I'm the one with an interest in exploring, remember. It could make my career."

"Mine too. If I can come up with a solid theory . . ."

"You don't need to go to Oxford to do that. I'll go and you stay home. I'm just as capable of buying a slide rule. I've got my credit card—oh!" Baffled, Jodie fell silent.

Charlotte, distressed by their argument, quickly intervened. "You cannot go today anyway. We must decide on a story to tell Roland, though I cannot like to deceive him." She glanced at Giles, who had returned to his formulae and was not listening. "*He* will have to be a long-lost cousin."

"From America," Emily suggested.

"I'm getting chilly," Jodie said. "Let's go in the bedroom, folks, and I'll get dressed. He'll never miss us."

Charlotte and Emily were fascinated by her bra and

pantyhose, but she steered them ruthlessly back to the subject at hand as she put on a borrowed gown.

"How do we explain my presence?"

"You must be Cousin Giles's sister." Charlotte was positive. "For propriety's sake. If I had known last night, I should *never* have allowed you to share these apartments." She cast a reproachful glance at Emily, who blushed.

"It was my fault," Jodie hastened to take the blame. "You need not worry, he is a perfect gentleman."

"In some situations, no gentleman is perfect, and in any case it is improper. Yes, you must be brother and sister."

"We don't look at all alike."

"Half-brother and -sister then."

"Lord Byron!" said Emily in a strangled whisper.

"Pray do not repeat gossip, Emily. If anyone should ask, we shall say that after Cousin Giles's mother's death, your father married a Red Indian. That will explain your black hair."

Jodie collapsed in laughter. "As a matter of fact, I am part Chinese, but I guess Native American will do."

"Jodie," mused Charlotte. "That is bound to make people ask questions. We shall introduce you as Judith." Her firm tone silenced Jodie's objection. "You lost your luggage on the way from America, and were robbed by a pickpocket in Oxford." She went on to detail how she would deal with the servants.

"Very ingenious," Jodie applauded. "A splendid plan."

Her face pink with pleasure at the compliment, Charlotte asked anxiously, "Do you suppose Cousin Giles will agree?"

"Agree?" said Jodie in astonishment. "He doesn't have a choice. He opted out of the planning so he'll just have to put up with whatever we say. He's a reasonable man."

"Things must be very different in your time. I would never dare tell Roland what to do, though sometimes I can coax him. I was distressed to hear you disputing with Cousin Giles."

"You'd better get used to it." Jodie's dark eyes held a martial sparkle. "I'm not about to lie around like a doormat for him to wipe his feet on. Let's go tell him our story."

Giles was far too involved in his equations to object to anything other than being dragged away from them to change his clothes. Jodie thought he looked great in the late viscount's knee-breeches and frock coat—he was too tall to borrow from Roland—but Emily shook her head.

"Shockingly old-fashioned," she said.

Jodie and Giles exchanged a glance and burst out laughing.

"She is right," Charlotte said. "You must order new clothes when you go into Oxford for your mathematical device."

"These are fine," Giles protested. "I can't repay you, so I don't want to spend more than I really have to."

"Jodie, pray tell him he must buy decent raiment," Charlotte appealed. "Roland never quibbles about paying my bills."

"You tell him. After all, you are his great-grandmother."

She blushed but went on gamely, "I cannot allow my husband's long-lost cousin to wear a coat twenty years out of date and shoes with huge silver buckles."

Giles threw a mischievous glance at Jodie. "We'll just say American fashions lag twenty years behind Europe's."

"Odious wretch," Jodie said, recalling the phrase from the Regency romances that had sparked her interest in history. "However, since I am able to wear Emily's clothes at least one of us shall uphold the honour of America, so if you want to go around looking like Benjamin Franklin, go ahead."

"Benjamin Franklin!" Giles yelped. "I've got much more hair and much less waistline, though an equal interest in lightning." He turned to Emily. "Is there a lightning rod on the stables?"

"Several. The old stables were burned down in a storm and Roland had a number of lightning rods built into the new stables. There is something special about them; I cannot remember what."

"I must see them." He headed for the nursery door.

"Not now!" Jodie called him back. "Charlotte has to get the servants out of the way so that we can arrive again."

She wondered how anyone so timid towards her husband

could possibly rule a houseful of servants, but Charlotte seemed to know what she was doing. She had already trusted her personal maid and Emily's with part of the story, since they had provided the clothes. To explain her visit to the unused nursery, she had told the housekeeper, Mrs. Briggs, she intended to refurbish it.

Now Jodie and Giles were hidden in a spare chamber, where Emily's abigail, Dinah, pinned up Jodie's hair in a respectable coiffure. Meanwhile, Charlotte dispatched the footman to Thame on an invented errand and sent all the housemaids to clean out the nursery. Once they were out of the way, she went to the housekeeper's room to consult her and the butler about the redecorating.

Emily and Dinah smuggled Giles and Jodie down to the front hall, and Charlotte's abigail, Matty, went to announce their pretended arrival to her mistress.

"They swallowed it hook, line, and sinker," Jodie whispered to Charlotte as she followed her into the drawing room. "You were splendid. You ought to be on the stage."

"On the stage!"

"Oh, sorry. I forgot actresses are not respectable. I'm going to have to learn to think before I speak."

"Yes, do be careful," said Charlotte worriedly. "Emily and I will do our best to teach you and Cousin Giles how to go on, but we have only a day and a half. I fear Roland and Lord Thorncrest may not be so easily taken in as Potter and Mrs. Briggs. I dread to think what Roland will do if he suspects we are deceiving him, yet I do not dare tell him all."

Jodie was beginning to dislike the present Lord Faringdale excessively.

= 3 =

REMINDED OF THE Earl of Thorncrest's impending arrival, Emily lost her animation. Listlessly she drifted to a sofa and sat drooping. Jodie joined her.

"Why do you not want to marry this Thorncrest?" she asked. "Only because he is a friend of Byron's?"

"Is that not enough?" Emily glanced at Charlotte, but she was talking to Giles. "They say Lady Caroline Lamb wrote in her diary that Lord Byron is 'mad, bad, and dangerous to know,'" she whispered. "I have heard that he mistreated his wife until she ran away, and that his half-sister is his mistress!"

"That is probably true," Jodie conceded, "but what has that to do with Lord Thorncrest? He is not a widower, is he?"

"No, he is a single gentleman."

"Then he cannot be accused of mistreating a wife. Has he a half-sister?"

"I believe not. But I have heard that he is a shocking rake, and besides his manner is so cutting that I am dreadfully afraid of him. He makes me feel a complete ninnyhammer."

"You have met him then. I thought Roland was forcing you to marry a complete stranger."

"We went to London for the Little Season last year and I met him there. I cannot imagine why he should wish to marry me, unless for my dowry."

"Surely your brother would not wed you to a fortune-hunter!"

"No, the earl is wealthy, but my portion would be a

splendid addition to any fortune. My great-grandfather, the first viscount, made a great deal of money in the South Sea Bubble, and in a hundred years it has grown considerably."

Jodie remembered that Giles was, as he had put it, "rather well-off," sufficiently well-off to refuse a salary for tax reasons. The Faringdales, it seemed, were an unusually thrifty lot, succeeding generations conserving and increasing the family fortune rather than dissipating it.

She glanced around the drawing room. The furnishings were a mixture of styles, from heavy Queen Anne cabinets carved with birds and fruit to the light, spare lines of Sheraton chairs. Jodie recognized several pieces from the museum part of the twentieth–century Waterstock Manor. Nothing had been discarded for the expensive sake of changing fashion, but everything was in excellent condition.

The gown she wore, and Emily's, and Charlotte's, though simple were of good quality, showing no signs of wear. And Charlotte had said that Roland never quibbled over her bills. Whatever his faults, Jodie regretfully acquitted the present Lord Faringdale of meanness. There were plenty of other charges against him.

"Roland cannot literally force you to marry Lord Thorndale, can he?" she asked Emily. "If he dragged you to the altar, the parson would refuse to conduct the ceremony."

"He can make my life miserable with his scolding, and it would be horrid for Charlotte, too. He would be bound to think she had supported me if I rebelled. Besides, it is my duty to obey him. I shall have to marry Lord Thorncrest." Tears welled in Emily's brown eyes.

"Do not despair yet," said Jodie bracingly. "You and Charlotte really must learn to stand up to these dictatorial men. It looks as if we are going to be here for a while yet, so I shall give you a few lessons in women's lib. Okay? I mean, all right?"

"Women's lib?"

"Well, we'll stick to assertiveness training. Standing up for your own opinions, and how to say no, that sort of stuff. I expect it would cause a few of Giles's paradoxes if we went out to fight for the vote."

His attention caught by his name, Giles heard the last part of Jodie's sentence. "Fight for the vote? Ye gods, Jodie, you wouldn't!"

"It seems a pity to pass up the opportunity," she said innocently. "I'm inclined to believe Dr. Brown's Conservation of Reality theory."

"In minor matters, yes, but something like that would have to change the future—our past—in a big way." Dismayed, Giles ran his fingers through his hair.

"You think I might succeed in winning the vote for women a century early? I'm flattered by your confidence in me. More likely my efforts would fizzle out and not make the slightest difference, but you needn't worry, I don't intend to try. I told Emily it would probably cause one of your paradoxes."

He sighed in relief. "So you were just teasing. I might have guessed. All the same, the longer we stay, the more likely something will go wrong. I must get back to work. Cousin Emily, will you take me to see the lightning rods on the stables? Don't worry, Jodie," he forestalled her protest with a grin. "We'll say that as a fellow-countryman and fellow-scientist of Ben Franklin's, I'm eager to see how the English have improved upon his invention."

Emily was glad to be distracted from her woes. As she and Giles left, the elderly butler came in with a tray of refreshments. Jodie eyed the tea and cakes hungrily. Since a snack lunch in Oxford yesterday, if yesterday was the right word, she had eaten nothing but what Emily had managed to smuggle up to them.

However, it was a long time since she had used the chamber pot in the night nursery.

"I don't suppose there's a water closet at Waterstock Manor?" she asked Charlotte without much hope. Probably the thrifty Faringdales considered such a luxury an unnecessary extravagance.

"My father-in-law had Burmah water closets installed years ago, two for the family and one for the servants. Shall I show you the way?"

At first glance the water closet looked like a superior outhouse—a polished wooden bench with a hole in it. However, underneath the bench was a porcelain bowl, and overhead hung a metal water tank for flushing just like the one in Jodie's Oxford digs two hundred years in the future.

Charlotte also showed her the separate bathroom, complete with shower bath. "Just tell Matty or Dinah when you want to bathe, so that the boiler can be stoked," she said.

"Heavenly!" Remembering last evening, Jodie giggled. "Giles will be thrilled to death. He had no appreciation of the historical significance of the chamber pot."

They returned to the drawing room and settled down for a comfortable cose.

"I like the way you joke with Cousin Giles," Charlotte said wistfully, as she poured the tea. "You must have known him a long time."

Jodie felt her cheeks grow warm. "As a matter of fact, I only met him yesterday. People in our time, especially Americans, tend to be much more free and easy with new acquaintances than here and now. Not that I would have accepted a ride with any man, even in England. I liked him right away, and felt I could trust him."

"He seems to be a—a great-grandson to be proud of. All the same, even though you are posing as his sister, I beg you will be careful how you behave with him. It seems young ladies in the future have little care for their reputations, but if you are going to be with us for some time, I should not like to see yours besmirched."

"You're a dear, Charlotte. With you to teach me, I shall do very well."

"I shall do my best. You already speak much more as we do than you did at first."

Jodie explained her interest in the Regency period. Charlotte was astonished that Jodie was a serious historian, and fascinated by the notion that her own times were the foundation for a whole genre of romantic novels. She confessed to a weakness for Minerva Press romances.

"It was Emily's idea to read Voltaire." Charlotte sighed. "She is much cleverer than I, but I fear it will do her no good with Lord Thorncrest. Gentlemen do not appreciate intelligence in a female."

Discussion of that interesting subject was postponed, as Emily and Giles returned. Giles's fair hair was ruffled, his blue eyes alight with excitement. Jodie found his enthusiasm endearing. If she had to be marooned in the past, there was no one she had rather be marooned with.

"I'm certain that's it," he told her. "The rods are built into the walls and they must still be there in our time. It's a most unusual configuration, with all of them grounding not more than two meters from where the accelerator will be. We were standing directly between the two! A thunderstorm produces enormous currents so a direct hit . . . I must get my papers."

Giles was ensconced in the library, from which he had to be pried like a winkle from its shell at mealtimes. The servants, told that he was a scientific gentleman, regarded him with a sort of awed indulgence that amused Jodie.

Charlotte had much the same attitude towards him. He was exempted from the rigorous instruction in etiquette to which she subjected Jodie. Jodie had to admit that his education as an English gentleman, together with the greater license permitted the male sex, probably justified Charlotte's trust.

On the other hand, her own knowledge of history helped her to learn quickly. She kept notes on everything, both to refresh her memory next day and for future use. Naturally graceful, she mastered curtsying with ease, much as she disapproved of the practice. Though she fell into bed exhausted and slept like a log, she woke next morning confident of her ability to deceive Roland and Lord Thorncrest.

In fact, despite Charlotte's lessons on the submissive behaviour proper to a young lady, Jodie was eager to cross swords with both gentlemen.

As the morning passed, Emily grew more and more agitated. It was almost a relief when at last the footman popped his head round the living room door to announce:

"His lordship's carriage is come, my lady."

"Thank you, Frederick." Charlotte rose, looking anxious. "Pray inform Mr. Faringdale. Jodie, you and Giles wait here as we arranged. Come, Emily."

"They cannot bite your head off," Jodie whispered to Emily, squeezing her hand. "Be brave."

Emily gave her a quavering smile and reluctantly trailed out into the hall after her sister-in-law as the footman went through the connecting door to the library to warn Giles.

Jodie very much wanted to watch the meeting. She contented herself with standing by the hall door so that she could see Charlotte and Emily but not be seen by the gentlemen, she hoped. To her surprise, Roland's greeting to his wife and sister sounded genuinely solicitous, if fussy. He kissed their cheeks, moving into Jodie's line of sight. Hastily she stepped back—and landed on Giles's foot.

"Ouch!" he whispered, steadying her. "What are we being surreptitious about?"

"I want to listen without being seen," she whispered back, moving forward again. "Hush."

"Nosy. Come and sit down like a good girl."

If his firm hand on her arm was not enough to persuade her, at that moment Lord Thorncrest straightened from bowing to Emily and caught her eye in a mirror she had not noticed. He raised one black eyebrow.

Jodie instantly yielded to Giles's tug and retreated, pink-cheeked.

"Drat," she said, sitting beside him on a sofa by the fire, "I wanted to hear what Charlotte said about us. I'm afraid the earl saw me."

"Serves you right for eavesdropping. Don't worry, it won't spoil our story. He'll just think you an inquisitive young lady. Correctly."

She pulled a face at him and he grinned.

Warned by footsteps, they stood up as Charlotte led her husband into the drawing room, followed by Emily and Lord Thorncrest. Jodie carefully avoided looking at the earl.

Curtsying to the present Lord Faringdale, she examined him with interest. The resemblance to the future Lord Faringdale was immediately obvious, though Roland was shorter than Giles, stockier, his eyes a paler blue and his hair a darker blond. He wore a worried expression like a badge of office—here was the head of the family, a man with weighty problems on his mind.

Perhaps because the addition of new family members increased the consequence of his position, he accepted Charlotte's introductions with complacency.

"How d'ye do, Miss Judith." He bowed to Jodie, then shook Giles's hand. "Cousin, I'm happy to make your acquaintance. From the Colonies, my wife tells me. Former colonies, I should say. Thorncrest, allow me to present my American cousins."

Jodie almost gasped as she curtsied to the earl. He was startlingly handsome, dark, with an arrogant nose, cynical mouth and determined chin. Hair as black as her own curled crisply and his piercing eyes held a disturbing glint. Bowing, he raised one eyebrow quizzically in an intentional reminder that she had been caught snooping. To her intense annoyance, she felt herself blush.

No wonder poor Emily was out of her depth. Jodie saw that she had taken a seat in an out-of-the-way corner, her head bowed over a piece of embroidery.

Jodie had no intention of being intimidated. "How do you do, my lord," she said sweetly, before adding a deliberate provocation. "You are an earl? We have abolished titles in the States, of course. Cousin Charlotte explained your English feudal system, but I fear I have forgotten—you are one rank above a duke, are you not?"

"Two below, Miss Judith," he replied promptly, looking amused rather than angry at being forced to admit his relative unimportance.

Roland, however, was as disconcerted as if a kitten had opened its mouth and roared like a lion, and Charlotte sent Jodie a glance of appeal.

"Why, Jodie, I'm surprised you do not remember," Giles intervened, his voice full of barely suppressed laughter. He went on, "My sister has the greatest admiration for the English peerage. She's been begging me for years to bring her to see our ancestral home.

27

"Nonsense, Giles," said Jodie indignantly, "you were just as keen as I."

Giles and Lord Thorncrest laughed, while Roland frowned. Jodie saw the viscount glance at Emily, alarmed lest she be tempted to emulate this piece of sisterly impertinence. Quiet in her corner, she did not appear to have heard.

Lord Thorncrest took the offensive. "Miss Judith, your speech is very different from your brother's. Your American accent is much stronger than Mr. Faringdale's, if you will forgive my mentioning it."

As if an American accent were an unmentionable disease, Jodie fumed, but she had no ready answer. Charlotte, too, looked blank.

Once again, Giles stepped into the breach. "I was lucky enough as a child to have an English governess," he said, his eyes daring Jodie to disavow his words. "Unfortunately, she returned home before Jodie was old enough to profit by her example."

"Ah, I see," the earl murmured, adding just loud enough for Jodie to hear, "no doubt that is sufficient explanation for her . . . manners."

Jodie had to admit to herself that he had drawn first blood. Worse was to come. Charlotte, in an attempt to forestall further questions about the differences between brother and sister, launched into an explanation of Jodie's supposed Red Indian ancestry.

By the time she finished her noble effort, Roland looked distinctly uneasy. Lord Thorncrest merely raised his quizzing glass and studied Jodie with a sardonic air.

"For all the world as if I were a savage!" Jodie stormed to Emily. The gentlemen had gone up to remove their travel dirt, Charlotte accompanying her husband, and Giles had returned to the library.

"It makes me want to run away when he looks at me like that," Emily confessed.

"It makes me want to hit him, the MCP."

"MCP?"

"Male chauvinist pig. What a pity that he is so handsome it takes your breath away."

"I do not care for dark men," said Emily positively. "Let us not talk about him. It makes me feel ill. Tell me what a male chauv—chauvinist?—pig is."

"All right, but come over by the fire. I'm cold." She led the way to the sofa by the fireplace.

Their discussion of the characteristics of the species lasted until the gentleman who had initiated it rejoined them. As he crossed the room, Jodie noted that his physique was as devastating as the face that had mesmerized her at first sight. Tall, broad-shouldered, lithe, he moved with the powerful grace of a mountain lion. The understated elegance of his close-fitting blue coat, modest shirt points, neat but plain cravat, and fawn pantaloons merely accentuated the virile strength within.

Quite a hunk, but she'd be damned if she'd let him know it.

Emily made a move as if to stand up and curtsy. Jodie's mind raced over Charlotte's etiquette instructions. Lord Thorncrest was both older and of higher rank, but as a suitor surely he did not rank such a courtesy. Jodie put her arm about Emily's waist and held her down.

"A sight as charming as it is improbable." The earl stood by the hearth, regarding them with a lazy smile. "Beauty and friendship combined."

"Improbable?" enquired Jodie.

"In my experience, beauty gives rise to jealousy more often than to amity."

"Then I must assume that you are flattering us, sir, when you call us beautiful, since our friendship is most sincere."

He laughed. "On the contrary, Miss Judith. I said improbable, not impossible. May I be seated, Miss Faringdale?"

"Of c-course, my lord," Emily stammered, crimsoning. "I . . . we . . . Luncheon will be served shortly."

"I am delighted to hear it. I find that travelling always gives me an appetite, do not you?"

"Yes. No. I mean . . ."

Jodie came to the rescue. "Do you live far from here, my lord?"

"Some thirty miles, ma'am. A mere nothing to one who has crossed the Atlantic Ocean."

Anxious to avoid questions about the nonexistent voyage, Jodie interrogated Lord Thorncrest about the state of the roads, the type of carriage he drove, the countryside through which he had passed.

"I cry mercy, Miss Judith," he protested at last. "It is plain that you are an eager student of all things English."

"If one does not learn from the experience, there is little point in travelling." In space or time, Jodie added silently. "I shall keep a journal that will be both interesting and useful when I return home."

"Then you mean to go back to America. That will be a great loss to all of us, will it not, Miss Faringdale?"

"Oh yes!"

He raised his expressive eyebrows at the fervour of Emily's response. She flushed again, and took a sudden, intense interest in her embroidery.

Charlotte and Roland came in, followed by Frederick who announced that a luncheon buffet was served in the morning room. They proceeded thither, and the ladies were seated while the gentlemen served them from the array of cold meats and pies, cheeses and fruits. Jodie would have preferred to help herself, particularly when she saw the delicate portions Lord Thorncrest considered suited to a ladylike appetite.

The gentlemen sat down.

"Potter, where is Mr. Giles?" enquired Roland, displeased. "I trust Frederick did not fail to inform him?"

"Certainly not, my lord." The butler was offended at the suggestion that his underling might be derelict in his duty. "Mr. Giles requested a tray in the library, being, I understand, at a crucial point in his calculations."

"Cousin Giles is prodigious dedicated to his science," said Charlotte anxiously.

"Ah yes, of course." Presented with a sufficient reason for the defection from his board, Roland was restored to equanimity. "What precisely is your brother studying, cousin?" he asked Jodie.

"Electricity. Pray do not ask me more, for I am sure it is beyond my poor brain to understand it. Giles is a disciple of Mr. Benjamin Franklin."

"Which no doubt accounts for his curious costume," murmured Lord Thorncrest *sotto voce.*

"Giles has more important matters on his mind than fashion." Jodie was annoyed.

"I beg your pardon, Miss Judith." The earl sounded more amused than contrite. "I spoke without thinking and meant no disrespect for your brother. Forgive me and smile on me, for your frown quite dashes me to the ground."

He continued to flatter her in an ironical way throughout the meal. Jodie discovered the pleasures of a light flirtation with an expert. Much to her annoyance she learned that a male chauvinist pig could, if he tried, make one feel delightfully feminine.

=== 4 ===

JODIE WAS IN Emily's dressing room, trying to decide which gown to borrow to wear for dinner, when Charlotte came in.

"Emily, I have persuaded Roland not to press for a formal betrothal until you have had time to come to know Thorncrest a little better. It is the best I can do. He is quite adamant that you shall marry him in the end."

"Bless you, Charlotte." Emily hugged her sister-in-law. "Who knows what may happen in a week or two. Perhaps he will decide he does not like me after all. He certainly acts as if he likes Jodie better."

There was no jealousy, only hope, in her voice. Nonetheless, Jodie was beginning to form a plan to improve relations between the two.

Lord Thorncrest was impatient with Emily's timidity, and amused by Jodie's boldness. Therefore Emily must learn to stand up for herself. On the other hand Emily was dead to the earl's undoubted charm, but if Jodie continued to encourage him to show his better side surely Emily would come to recognize it. And if, meanwhile, Lord Thorncrest made plain a decided preference for Jodie, it would be only natural for Emily to begin to feel a bit envious, if not outright jealous.

Her head whirling with plots, Jodie chose a gown at random and hurried to her chamber to scramble into it. It would take time for her plan to bear fruit, and she had no idea how long she had. She fidgeted while Dinah re-pinned her hair, then dashed down to the library.

Giles was lounging back in his chair with his feet on

Roland's desk, along with a neat stack of papers.

"Very pretty," he said approvingly, smiling at her.

She looked down at the canary-yellow crape with its rows of ruffles at the hem. "It is, isn't it?" She settled Emily's white cashmere shawl about her shoulders. "I always did like Regency fashions."

"Yes, the dress is attractive, but it was you I meant."

"Why, thank you, kind sir." She bobbed a curtsy. "I see *you* are still twenty years out of date."

"And growing very tired of this coat, to say nothing of the shoes, which pinch abominably. Charlotte wins, I shall have to buy some clothes."

"We're going to be here for quite a while, I take it. Have you done all the figuring you can without a slide rule?"

"Just about, though what stopped me now is that this blasted oil lamp Frederick brought me seems to produce more smoke than light. You're the historian, can you do something about it?"

"Yes, we used to use—will use?—them for barbecues, filled with citronella oil to keep away the bugs." She carefully turned the wick down a little, then sat on the edge of the desk. "It's nearly dinner time anyway, so don't start work again. I take it you're planning to go to Oxford tomorrow?"

"Do I sense a challenge there?" Giles teased. "I shan't try to stop you going with me. I've been thinking about the Conservation of Reality law, and it makes a lot of sense. As long as we're careful I don't see why we shouldn't go out and about."

"Good."

"You know, the implications of this whole thing are enormous," he said. "Emily's talk of *Micromégas* yesterday made me think that there may be applications to space flight. If we ever succeed in travelling near the speed of light, time dilation will be a significant problem."

"Space travel! For Pete's sake, Giles, concentrate on getting us home. You can figure out the rest when you get back to your computers."

"Don't worry, I haven't actually done any work on it. It just made me wonder, when Cassandra Brown's theory has so many fascinating implications, why she threw the whole thing up and disappeared. . . . Ye gods, you don't suppose the same thing happened to her?"

"You mean she might have been thrown back through time like us?"

"She resigned, completely out of the blue, and had her stuff sent to M.I.T. That's where she took her doctorate. But when I wrote to her there with a couple of questions, my letter was returned. No one seems—seemed—will seem?—to know where she went."

"But if she took precautions like that, it sounds as if she intended to leave. Surely she wouldn't have travelled to the past deliberately?"

"She might have, to test her theory. No family to worry about, I gather."

"Unlike you and me." Jodie had a sudden sinking feeling. Till now she had not really considered the possibility of being stranded in the past forever. Mom and Dad would be shattered if she vanished without a trace.

"Exactly." Giles, too, had family he cared about. "If I could get in touch with her, we could work together on returning to our present."

"She might be anywhere in time. Perhaps she went to the future."

"No, I believe there must be some connection with this particular segment of time. Some interdimensional space-time curve, perhaps. There's a good chance, I think, that if that's what happened to her she's not too far away."

"Where was her lab? You said near London. It might be worth writing to her, I guess, if you can figure out where to send the letter. Can't hurt, anyway."

"Luckily her lab was also in a stately home, believe it or not, though the family died out some time ago. Font House, in Kent." He swung his long legs off the desk, pulled a fresh sheet of paper towards him and dipped a quill in the standish. "No time like the present. This is going to have to be carefully worded in case someone else reads it. 'Dear Dr. Brown,' " he wrote.

"That's no good for a start. Women couldn't—can't—take

degrees, let alone doctorates. 'Dear Miss Brown'? 'Dear Cassandra Brown'? Perhaps you'd better just make it 'Madam,' and address it to Cassandra Brown without any title."

"Okay." Giles screwed up the paper, tossed it towards the fireplace, and started again. " 'Madam,'—let's see—'If you recognize the name signed below, you will doubtless understand the situation.' "

"That sounds suspiciously mysterious."

Again he crumpled the sheet, this time throwing it at Jodie. "All right, you dictate."

" 'Madam, We are two stranded travellers who beg the assistance of a fellow-exile. . . .' "

"Gothic, and bad Gothic at that."

"Don't tell me you read Gothics, Giles!"

"My sister Kate used to, and I picked one up by mistake."

"Mistake—ha. No one could mistake one of those covers. Okay, so that's bad Gothic. Let's try again. We'd better ask her to address her answer to me, so we don't have to explain about there being two Lord Faringdales."

The library floor was scattered with balls of paper by the time they agreed on sufficiently innocuous wording.

"Now where does Roland keep his envelopes?" Giles opened a desk drawer.

"No such thing yet. You fold it, write the address on the outside, and then seal it with wax," Jodie said, throwing the rejected sheets on the fire.

"That must be what these red sticks are. I hope you know what to do with the stuff."

Jodie had an excellent theoretical grasp of the use of sealing wax. She discovered that the practical application was another matter altogether. She and Giles were helpless with laughter over a smelly pool of congealing red liquid when Lord Thorncrest entered the library, elegant and impeccable in black and white.

"You don't use sealing wax in America?" he enquired, his eyebrows indicating disbelief.

"The composition must be different," Jodie gasped, trying to stop giggling.

"Allow me to assist."

"Thanks," said Giles, "but I'm going to have to recopy the letter anyway."

"Later then. Faringdale can frank it for you, of course, but if he is otherwise occupied I shall be glad to be of service."

Seeing Giles's blank look, Jodie said hastily, "Thank you, my lord. Giles, let us go and ask Cousin Roland if we may borrow a carriage to go into Oxford tomorrow."

"No doubt you wish to replace the wardrobe you lost at sea, Faringdale," said Lord Thorncrest as they went through to the drawing room. "Perhaps I can direct you to a tailor who is somewhat more conversant with modern modes than your American tailor appears to be."

His tone was bland, but Jodie was sure he had every intention of mocking. She was ready to flare up in Giles's defense when she caught his eye and he shook his head slightly. He looked amused.

"That's kind of you, my lord," he said mildly. "Perhaps you can also tell me where to go for scientific instruments. My slide rule was lost too."

"Slide rule? Ah yes, I believe I know what you mean. I fear I never could spare the time for playing with numbers when I was up at Oxford. I daresay your cousin might be able to advise you."

Roland was standing with his back to the drawing room fire, ostentatiously consulting his pocket watch. As they entered he nodded in satisfaction and put it away. "We dine in seven minutes," he announced. "You were saying that I might be able to advise my cousins, Thorncrest?"

"Faringdale needs some mathematical knickknack."

"This is ridiculous," said Jodie crossly, her ire at last finding an outlet. "You cannot go on calling both Giles and Cousin Roland 'Faringdale.' They both have perfectly good first names and surely you do too?"

"My given name is Charles, Miss Judith. I trust it meets with your approval." He was sarcastic.

"Charlie," mused Jodie, noting from the corner of her eye Roland's apoplectic face. "Or better yet, Chuck."

"Judith, I must absolutely forbid you to address the earl

by his Christian name," Roland burst out, "whatever your heathen American custom."

"Indeed, it would not be proper, Jodie," Charlotte agreed, scandalized.

Unexpectedly Lord Thorncrest laughed. "If propriety prevents my being called Chuck, then long live propriety. I believe you might be permitted to call me Thorncrest, however, Miss Judith." He turned to Giles. "Perhaps, to pacify your sister and avoid confusion, I had best use your Christian name?"

"By all means, Charles," Giles responded gravely.

The earl was visibly taken aback. Jodie realized that he had not expected to reciprocate by allowing an American nobody the freedom to use *his* first name. However, he could hardly object now. Giles had scored a point and, looking at him, Jodie saw by the glint in his blue eyes that he was well aware of it.

What ridiculous complications! It made the California custom of addressing all and sundry by their first names appear eminently sane.

To Roland's obvious relief, Potter announced dinner and they moved into the dining room. Charlotte set herself to smooth ruffled feathers all around. Between her gentle chatter of commonplaces and her cook's excellent meal, she succeeded admirably.

Roland unbent sufficiently to offer a choice of carriages for the outing to Oxford on the morrow. When Giles admitted that he could not drive, Thorncrest confined himself to a curled lip, forgoing the opportunity for sarcasm. And then Jodie, sitting next to Roland, pleased him with her interest in his country pursuits.

"Of course, our English way of doing things is not at all what you are used to," he said forgivingly, patting her hand. "If you will only heed Charlotte, you will soon learn. Charlotte is equal to anything." He beamed at his wife with such fond pride that Jodie was almost prepared to like him despite his pomposity.

Only Emily, seated beside her future husband, was as ill at ease as ever.

When the ladies withdrew at the end of the meal, Jodie was alarmed to see that Giles was about to follow them. However, Roland merely said jovially, "I hope you will join us for a glass of port, cousin. I should like your opinion on a particularly fine vintage I have been saving for a special occasion."

Giles turned back and sat down again, after a brief grimace for Jodie's eyes alone. She gathered that he was not fond of port.

"It's not fair," she complained as the door closed. "Being a man, he can get away with any mistakes on the grounds of being an American and an absentminded scientist, while everything I do is wrong."

"You are managing very well, is she not, Emily?" Charlotte encouraged her, but her worried air made Jodie feel guilty.

"I only wish I were managing half as well," said Emily unhappily. As Charlotte turned away to direct the footman in the placement of a card table, she added in a whisper, "I do admire your boldness, Jodie, though that is not at all what Charlotte means. I wish I dared to emulate it, if it would not distress Charlotte and Roland as I know it must."

"It would not suit you; you are by far too gentle-natured. There is no need, though, to go to the opposite extreme and be afraid of that wretched man."

Emily smiled. "As to that, I believe I am already less afraid after watching you stand up to him. One of these days, I shall even be able to think of a sensible answer when he speaks to me."

"Of course you will." Charlotte had heard her last words. "Jodie, do you play cards?"

"Only pinochle. My dad likes a game now and then."

"Oh dear, I have never heard of it. Still, if you do not object, I daresay Roland will like to teach you whist. Emily, I hope you will give us some music this evening?"

Glad of an excuse to avoid conversation, Emily went straight to the pianoforte and began to play. She had a light but expressive touch. Jodie enjoyed it, though she was no expert. She listened with pleasure as she went to the card table and began surreptitiously to remove certain cards from the packs, pretending to shuffle.

Charlotte followed her and dropped into one of the chairs. She was far too agitated to pay any attention to Jodie's activities.

"At last I can speak to you!" She clasped her hands and leaned forward. "Jodie, I do not know what to do. Roland thinks I am increasing."

"Increasing?" It took Jodie a moment to realize what she meant. "Pregnant? And you're not? Why should he—Oh no! You suddenly developed an interest in redecorating the nursery. I guess the servants could not wait to pass on the news."

Charlotte nodded. "I gather Mrs. Briggs told Roland's valet, and of course he told Roland. He is so delighted, I *cannot* disappoint him by telling him it is all a hum."

"Sh—darn—drat, what a mess. I suppose you'd better wait till your next period and tell him you were mistaken. When's it due?"

"Pray hush, Jodie!" Charlotte whispered, fiery-faced, glancing around nervously. "It—it will be three weeks; I have just—you know."

"Perhaps by then you really will be pregnant." Jodie patted her hand comfortingly. She remembered with relief that among the odds and ends she had bought in Oxford while searching for a transformer was a box of tampons. Rags, they used in 1816. Horrors!

At that inappropriate moment, the gentlemen came through from the dining room. Giles went straight to the piano and started turning pages for Emily. Roland fussed over Charlotte, asking if she was warm enough, if she would not like a more comfortable chair. Lord Thorncrest lounged against the mantel, his sardonic appraisal of the company suggesting to Jodie that he was unused to being one of a family party and did not care for the experience.

Under her husband's solicitude, Charlotte had regained her countenance. "I shall do very well here, Roland," she assured him. "I thought perhaps Lord Thorncrest might like to play a rubber of whist, if he does not mind being patient while Jodie learns the rules."

"It will be my pleasure, ma'am. Miss Judith, may I hope you will permit me the honour of teaching you?" The earl sauntered over to the card table.

Jodie waited until he had taken his seat before she answered. "Thank you, Thorncrest, but I have a better notion. I shall teach you all an American game."

Roland frowned. "Whist is a most refined pastime."

"But I have already sorted the cards." Jodie did her best to sound utterly cast down. She was not sure how to pout but she tried. She hoped her expression conveyed hurt disappointment. "You see, in pinochle you use only the cards from nine to ace." Metaphorically, she played her trump. "And I fear I cannot remember where I put the others."

They were on the floor, hidden by her skirts. Floor-length dresses had their uses after all.

"I'm always happy to learn a new card game." Lord Thorncrest actually sounded half-way enthusiastic.

Roland capitulated. Fortunately the cards fell his way and he won their practice round, which was quite enough to make him keen to continue.

As the earl shuffled, Jodie became aware that Giles was now playing the piano. He sounded even better than Emily and she wanted to listen.

"It would not be fair to take part in the next hand as I am so much more experienced," she said. "I shall sit it out and you can consult me at need."

Not waiting for Roland's inevitable expostulation she stood up, scattering the pile of surplus cards with her foot so that it would look as if they had been dropped accidentally. She moved to a nearby wing chair, pulled off her borrowed slippers, and curled up comfortably with her legs under her.

Giles was playing from memory, something that she thought must be Chopin. She had not known he was a pianist. Of course, she had only known him a couple of days, even if it seemed like forever. He was utterly intent on the music, as unaware of the world as when he was absorbed in his calculations. Jodie listened entranced, watching his long fingers dancing on the ivory keys.

She shivered as she remembered his touch on her back when he buttoned the now-vanished blouse.

"Cousin Judith, how many points are four knaves worth?"

"Knaves? Oh, jacks. Forty." Her mood was broken, and as if he guessed it Giles swung into a Scott Joplin rag.

Joplin! Jodie was not sure of the composer's dates but he was most certainly anachronistic, and she had a feeling Chopin was too. How could Giles be so careless? Luckily, only she and Emily had been paying any attention—but the syncopated rhythm of the rag was changing that.

Roland's foot tapped in time to the beat; Charlotte looked round in surprised dismay, relaxing when she saw it was not Emily playing; Lord Thorncrest raised his damning eyebrows.

"What *interesting* talents your cousin has, Faringdale," he observed. "One might almost suppose oneself in the street being annoy—entertained by a hurdy-gurdy."

Roland's enjoyment faded. He put down his cards and went over to the piano. Jodie could not hear what he said, but in any case his remonstrance had precisely no effect. Giles, throwing himself into a particularly tricky bit of the Maple Leaf Rag, did not even notice him. Roland turned away with a disconsolate shrug and stalked back towards the card table.

On the way, his outraged gaze fell on Jodie. He leaned down and hissed in her ear, "Ladies do not sit thus!"

Hastily she uncurled her legs and put on her slippers. There was no sense in giving the poor man an apoplexy.

= 5 =

As IF REPENTING of his overreaction the night before, Roland graciously granted Jodie's request to have Emily accompany herself and Giles into Oxford. They set off shortly after breakfast in the viscount's comfortable but unostentatious carriage, driven by his coachman and with Frederick up behind.

"Giles, much as I enjoyed it you *must* not play Scott Joplin," Jodie said at once.

He looked guilty. "I know. Sorry, I got carried away. What about Chopin? Emily, have you ever heard of Frédéric Chopin?"

Emily shook her head.

"I'm not much into Mozart and Haydn. What about Mendelssohn? Schubert?"

"Schubert sounds familiar, though I have not heard his music. I know, the Austrian boy-genius. Some call him a second Mozart."

"You're probably safe sticking to Schubert then," said Jodie.

"Forgive me," Emily said hesitantly, "but it might be better if Cousin Giles does not play at all in company. It is not quite the thing for gentlemen, unless perhaps in a private concert, or just for the family."

"Why on earth not?" Giles was indignant.

"She's right," Jodie agreed reluctantly. "It was okay in Georgian and Victorian times, but for a period in between it was considered odd for any man not a professional musician to play."

Giles sighed. "If you say so. I suppose I ought to concentrate on getting us home anyway."

"Writing poetry is much the same, is it not, Emily? It was—is not considered normal for a gentleman, though if you were a genius you might be lionized, like Lord Byron."

"Lord Byron is in disgrace," Emily reminded her. "Lady Byron has run home to her parents with her baby."

"I was reading about Ada Byron, the daughter, last night. I picked up a biography by chance in that used-book store on Broad Street. I expect you know it, Giles?"

"If you mean the second-hand book shop, yes," he teased. "But what were you doing reading a book about the future, when Roland has a whole library of contemporary books?"

"I was writing up my notes on the day until quite late, and as I was in my nightgown I thought I'd better not go down to the library so I read what I had to hand. Ada sounds like a pretty smart kid, but Annabella—Lady Byron—is altogether another kettle of fish. Self-righteous, tyrannical, determined to have her own way. She even fired Ada's nanny because Ada was getting too fond of her. Will fire her, rather."

"Fire?" queried Emily.

"Dismiss. She did encourage Ada to study math, but only because she thought it would squelch any tendency for her to be like her father. Lady Byron's a real hypochondriac too, always thinking she's at death's door, while Ada really was sick a lot. The poor kid's heading for a pretty miserable childhood."

"Calm down, Jodie," said Giles. "Despite your muddled tenses you sound quite upset. Do you always take everything you read so personally?"

Jodie had to laugh at herself. "No, of course not. I guess it's because here we are at the beginning of the story and it seems a pity that it's sort of all happened once already and it's going to happen again the same way. If you see what I mean. Also, I can't help being sorry for Lord Byron, whatever he did. He wants desperately to see his daughter before he goes into exile, and Annabella won't let him. And that's happening right now."

"You are a very kind person," said Emily seriously. "I can see why you sympathize with Lord Byron. Do you like his poetry? Roland says it is too shocking for me to read, but I know you are not so easily shocked."

Jodie laughed again. "Not easily shocked, but easily bored. To tell the truth, I have never managed to read more than a few lines of his epics, though some of the shorter poems are wonderful:

"She walks in beauty, like the night
Of cloudless climes and starry skies,
And all that's best of dark and bright
Meets in her aspect and her eyes. . . ."

She leaned forward, peering out of the window. "Oh, Emily, can we stop and talk to that ploughman? I must have the perspective of an agricultural labourer for my thesis."

"Perspective?" Emily wrinkled her forehead in puzzlement. "You want to sketch him?"

"Interview him," Giles explained. "Not now, Jodie. He'll likely lose his wits at being hailed by a beautiful young lady in an elegant carriage. You'd do better to visit one of the local farmers. Besides, we have a lot to do in Oxford."

"Okay." Jodie sat back with a sigh that was not as heavy as it might have been had he not called her a beautiful young lady. She hoped he meant it.

They accomplished all their errands in Oxford, though Giles was disappointed with the slide rule he bought. Apparently no one had yet got around to inventing a cursor for it, so the types of calculation it would help with were limited. Nonetheless, he retired to the library with it as soon as they reached Waterstock Manor.

Charlotte was busy about some household task. Roland and Lord Thorncrest were still out shooting—at what Jodie squeamishly did not ask. Joining Giles in the library, she settled at a small writing table to put down her impressions of Oxford in 1816 before they faded from her mind. Emily came in, took a book from the shelves, and curled up in the corner of a large sofa.

44

It was growing dark. Frederick came to make up the fire, lit several branches of candles and went out again. For some time there was no sound but the scratching of quill pens, the rustle of paper and the crackling of the fire.

Candle flames wavered as the door opened. Lord Thorncrest entered. His colour heightened by fresh air and exercise, he looked particularly handsome and seemed for once to be satisfied with the world.

Emily gasped and hurriedly uncurled, dropping her book on the floor in the process. Jodie saw her move her skirt to cover it and wondered what reprehensible work she was reading now.

"We had a splendid day's sport," the earl announced. "Your brother is to be congratulated on his coverts, Miss Faringdale. Do you shoot, Giles?"

Giles looked up vaguely. "Did someone say something?"

"I asked if you shoot."

"Oh yes, occasionally. Excuse me, Charles, I'm right in the middle of rather a complex equation." Before he finished his sentence his attention had returned to his numbers.

Lord Thorncrest grinned at Jodie. "I see you are hard at work too, Miss Judith, writing your journal, no doubt. What frightful things do you have to say about us feudal English?"

"Nothing kind," she retorted. "No, as a matter of fact, I am simply describing Oxford at present. I drew your character last night."

"Alas, I fear I should be quite set down were I to read it. What think you, Miss Emily?" He moved to join her on the sofa. "Ah, you have dropped your book."

She bent to pick it up, but he stooped swiftly and reached it first. He read the title and his eyebrows rose, but in surprise rather than disapproval, Jodie thought. She eavesdropped unrepentantly.

"Jean Jacques Rousseau, and in French. A curious choice for a lady of your years. What is your opinion of Monsieur Rousseau's works?"

"He writes beautifully," said Emily defiantly, "and his ideas are interesting, though not as well thought out as Voltaire's."

"Voltaire too! You have intellectual tastes. I daresay there is no room in your life for the novels of the Minerva Press?"

"I have read some," she admitted, pink-cheeked. "Charlotte likes them." She glanced round as the door opened and Roland came in. Dismayed, she blurted in an undertone, "Pray give me the book, sir!"

His look was understanding. "Better that I keep it," he said softly. "I shall not give you away."

Roland beamed his approval on seeing his sister sitting with the earl. "A good day, hey, Thorncrest? Giles, you must come out with us tomorrow. The partridge will start nesting soon and I don't shoot after that."

Jodie glared at Giles. She couldn't believe he would go out there and slaughter innocent birds for fun. Her glare had no more effect than Roland's words; Giles noticed neither. Roland chuckled indulgently and pulled up a chair beside Jodie.

"You are as diligent with your journal, Cousin, as Giles with his studies."

For a moment Jodie thought he was going to exercise his authority and insist on reading her papers. She was glad she had foreseen the possibility and written in a style appropriate to the period. However, he decided against it. Perhaps he was learning caution in his dealings with her.

"I see your shopping expedition was successful," he went on, nodded towards Giles, who was now clad in swallow-tail coat and pantaloons and wielding a slide rule.

"Thanks to you, Cousin Roland. We cannot be sufficiently grateful for your generosity."

His chest puffed visibly. "As head of the family, I consider it my responsibility to see that all are provided for, from replacing your lost belongings to planning a superior match for my sister."

"Even if she cannot like it?"

"A young girl cannot be expected to understand how to choose a husband who will make her happy."

"Did not Charlotte choose to marry you?"

"Dear me, no. What odd notions you Americans have! My dear Charlotte's father and I arranged the matter between us, and see how splendidly it has turned out."

46

To that, Jodie had no response.

Satisfied to have gained his point, as he thought, Roland left her to her journal and went to take a seat near Emily and Lord Thorncrest. Jodie resumed her eavesdropping.

"You have an excellent library here, Faringdale," observed the earl. "I discovered some volumes of Rousseau on the shelves and I have just now been recommending his works to Miss Emily."

"Rousseau! Emily!" Roland's face was such a picture of horror that Jodie found it difficult not to laugh.

"His writing is a model of clarity in the French language, do you not agree? And it cannot but be instructive to compare his philosophy with that of his arch-enemy, Voltaire. I trust you possess a set of Voltaire's works also?"

"Yes, I believe so, that is . . . It cannot be right to expose an innocent girl to the seditious ideas of Voltaire and Rousseau."

"You think not? What is your opinion, Miss Emily?"

Emily cast a timid glance from her brother to her suitor and back. There was no way out, she must disagree with one of them.

"Since Lord Thorncrest is so good as to advise me, Roland, I feel I ought to accept his advice."

As his lordship handed over the book, Jodie just managed not to clap and cry Bravo! She was surprised that the earl had taken the trouble to do so much for Emily. A moment's reflection suggested that he was animated by a malicious desire to bait the brother rather than any wish to please the sister. Still, he had taken some notice of her for once. Perhaps if Emily learned to face up to him he might learn to appreciate her for more than her looks, her money, and her distinguished family tree.

Jodie watched them that evening and the next morning. Though Lord Thorncrest did not use his cutting tongue on Emily, nor did he evince any interest in her beyond the most formal courtesy. According to Charlotte, he and Roland were determined upon the match, but he made no apparent attempt to woo his prospective bride.

Too sure of himself by half, Jodie decided.

She saw little of Giles that day. He went riding with Lord Thorncrest while Roland was busy about some urgent estate business, and Jodie went with Emily to visit a local farm. Later, after changing for dinner, she ran Giles to earth in the usual place.

"I hope you did not shoot anything," she said severely.

Giles looked up from his papers and said with forced cheerfulness, "No, one does not shoot while riding, and in any case I prefer target shooting. Was your expedition successful?"

"Excessively successful. The farm people were celebrating a christening—Emily took the baby a silver mug—and I have a vast quantity of information about partying down on the farm. I believe I shall narrow my topic to leisure activities in town and country. Emily is a great help to me. She is such a dear, and highly intelligent. Do you not think that Thorncrest might come to realize what a treasure she is?"

"I'd like to think so, but I'm afraid he was telling me only this afternoon that all he is looking for is a complaisant wife. His father died eighteen months ago and he is prepared to do his duty by marrying and begetting an heir but his wife means so little to him that he doesn't care if she is a bluestocking—his words, not mine! There's no need to look daggers at me. He doesn't believe Emily actually understands what she's reading anyway."

"Are you serious? Okay, if you ever decide to do some shooting, you have my permission to use the earl as a target. I'm surprised he told you all this."

"I have gone up vastly in his estimation since he saw me on horseback. I'm quite a good rider."

"Knowing your talent for understatement, I assume that means you're a champion steeplechaser. I hope this means that he will stop treating you in that odiously mocking way. How can you let him get away with it?" Jodie was indignant at the memory.

Giles reached for her hand. "Calm down. Would you rather I reacted to every jibe by trying to prove my worth? I don't need to, Jodie. His opinion of me is unimportant. Wasn't it your home state, California, that set up a commission on self-esteem?" He smiled teasingly. "Well, my self-esteem is in very good shape, thank you."

She clung to his hand, suddenly grateful for his assurance, his belief in himself. Depending on him absolutely, she needed his confidence in his own dependability. Her faith was not shaken even when he laughed ruefully and admitted that he had reached *point non plus* in his calculations.

"At the moment I'm working on reinventing the slide rule. I can't do much more without a more advanced version. It's going to take a while."

"You'll do it. And besides, I am enjoying myself prodigiously and I'm in no hurry to go home."

"Beware, you're going native. I wonder if that's what happened to Dr. Brown. I would not have come here deliberately without bringing all the calculations necessary to return home, and a calculator for last minute adjustments."

"She might not be here at all, or she might have come by accident like us, or she might have got into some sort of trouble here, not having obliging relatives waiting."

"Or she might have chosen to stay. How long does the postal service take these days?"

"Better than in our time. Kent's the other side of London, isn't it? Two days max to get there, allowing for sorting in London, and two days back. Of course, she might not be at Font House or she might decide not to answer."

"I think she would answer. I only met her once and I can't say I know her well, but though she was rather reserved she didn't strike me as the sort to refuse to help us. Keep your fingers crossed, Jodie. We badly need her help."

=== 6 ===

"THERE'S A LETTER for you, Miss Judith." Potter proffered a silver salver as Jodie and Emily entered the hall.

Jodie was tempted to leave it till later. They had been into Thame, to the Tuesday market. Her head was full of the bustling little town, its broad main street lined with houses and shops and inns, thatched, half-timbered, brick, stone, and stucco. Though the business of the day was the buying and selling of cattle and agricultural products, the weekly gathering served as an excuse for merrymaking. Jodie wanted to capture on paper the puppet show, the ballad singer, the boys with hoops, and the gossiping women.

But the letter could only be from one person. It was too important to be postponed.

"Is Mr. Faringdale in the library?"

"No, miss, I believe he went riding."

"Drat. Thank you, Potter. Come on, Emily, let's see what she has to say." Jodie led the way into the drawing room.

"Who is it from?" Emily was puzzled. "I did not know you were acquainted with anyone else in England. In this time, I mean."

Jodie explained about Dr. Brown as she pulled off her gloves. Picking up the letter again, she noticed that it had been franked by Lord Font. Her heart sank.

"We wrote to her at Font House," she said. "This is probably just a note from Lord Font saying she's never been heard of. How do I open this without ripping the whole thing?"

Emily fetched a paperknife and carefully slit the seal. Unfolding the sheet, Jodie looked at once at the signature.

"Cassandra Brown! Thank heaven." She sank into a chair. "She is living in London with a Lady Bestor, and will be happy to receive us there whenever convenient. Her letter's as cautious as ours was. Oh, she has signed it 'Mrs.'—but if she had married here she would not still be 'Brown'."

"Perhaps she is passing as a widow. That would make it much easier for a female on her own. I wonder who Lady Bestor is."

"Who knows." Jodie shrugged. "I wish Giles was here. We shall have to go to London."

"Let us go and tell Charlotte. I expect she is taking her enforced rest. Roland is so solicitous, it makes her feel horridly guilty." Emily had been let into the secret of Charlotte's supposed pregnancy, since Jodie hadn't the least regard for the impropriety of discussing such matters with an unmarried young lady.

Charlotte was reclining upon a daybed in her dressing room. She was delighted to see them and set down her book, *Mansfield Park*, without regret.

"It is very odd," she confided. "Why, the hero is a sadly ordinary clergyman, and Fanny is a poor little dab of a girl. All the characters might well be one's neighbours. There is nothing half so exciting in it as having Jodie and Giles appear from the future."

"The author is very much admired in the future," Jodie assured her.

"Oh, then I shall try to finish it. Did you enjoy seeing the market?"

"Very much, but we have come to tell you about this letter." Once again she explained about Cassandra Brown. "So you see, we must go to London."

"Perhaps Giles will want to go on his own."

"Let him just try! I need to research the amusements of the city. I suppose I shan't be able to gatecrash the *ton* parties, but there are plenty of other things to see."

Charlotte sat bolt upright. "I have a simply splendid notion! We shall all go. Then I shall be able to sponsor you to balls and routs and Emily can have a proper Season before she is married."

"Roland will never agree to it," said Emily wistfully.

"Yes, he will, for I mean to tell him that I want to consult a London doctor, and that only the best furnishings from the best shops are good enough for his heir's nursery. I am sorry to deceive him further, but sooner or later I shall really have a baby so it will not all be for nothing."

Jodie was struck by an unpleasant possibility. Suppose Charlotte never had the child she so confidently expected? Suppose she had died young and Roland remarried, making some unknown woman Giles's ancestor? Giles was as vague about his family tree as Roland had shown himself to be in accepting his unknown cousins. He was certain only that the direct line from father to son was unbroken. Where inheritance was concerned, mothers counted for nothing.

It did not bear thinking about. Jodie joined Emily in smothering Charlotte with hugs and kisses and congratulations on her brilliant plan, until she squeaked for mercy.

Emily's hopes flourished. "Perhaps I shall meet someone else Roland would consider a suitable husband."

"You know, Charlotte," said Jodie, "it could be a way out of your own problem too. You can tell Roland the doctor says you were mistaken about the pregnancy. But how are we going to explain Cassandra?"

"That is easy," Charlotte assured her. "You said she is American. Nothing could be more likely than that you have a letter of introduction to an American lady living in London. In fact, if Roland were suspicious of you, which he is not, that would be enough to abate his mistrust."

"Great. All right, you tackle Roland and I'll tell Giles. Boy, I can't wait to see the big city."

Giles was equally enthusiastic, though his reasons were quite different. Apart from his desire to return home and his concern over the dangers of their lengthening stay, he was eager to discuss the theory of time travel with someone who must know more about it than he did.

Used to more scintillating company, Lord Thorncrest also welcomed the suggestion that they should all go up to town. Vastly outnumbered, Roland conceded and sent a groom up to London with instructions to the staff of his town house to prepare for their arrival.

Three days later they were off. After the first few miles, Jodie found the journey excruciatingly tedious. She envied Giles, riding alongside. He looked splendid on horseback, sitting tall and straight yet relaxed, in contrast to Roland who somehow managed to appear pompous even in the saddle. Lord Thorncrest had driven ahead in his curricle, promising to call on them the next day as he had his own house in London. Jodie wished she could have gone with him, covering the fifty miles in four hours instead of the six or more Roland's travelling carriage would take.

"Oh no," said Charlotte when she mentioned this wish, "not on the post road. It is unexceptionable to drive with a gentleman in an open carriage about the country lanes, or in town, of course. Indeed, it is every young lady's desire to be driven in the park by an eligible gentleman."

"Then I shall have to coax Roland or Thorncrest to take me, as Giles does not drive. All in the way of research, you understand."

They stopped to take luncheon at the Saracen's Head in Beaconsfield. Jodie found the coaching inn fascinating. She tried to take notes when they set out again but the carriage, though comfortable and well-sprung, rocked too much. She had to acknowledge that it was almost equally impossible to write in a car on a freeway. Nonetheless, when at last they stiffly emerged from the vehicle onto the Mayfair sidewalk, she murmured, "Three cheers for Henry Ford."

The Faringdale townhouse was on Grosvenor Street, one of a row of Georgian brick façades joined in a terrace. Pilasters framed the front door, and the ground floor windows had curved pediments that reminded Jodie of Lord Thorncrest's raised eyebrows. On either side of the steps up to the entrance, ornamental ironwork separated the sidewalk—no, the pavement—from the sunken area. The kitchen and "domestic offices" would be down there in the basement. Jodie glanced down the steep stairway and was glad to see that at least the servants had plenty of light and air from large windows.

Whatever his faults, Roland treated his servants well. To her relief, she soon discovered that the family was equally well taken care of; like Waterstock Manor, the house had Burmah water closets.

A half hour later the travellers were comfortably ensconced in the back parlour, with a fire blazing against the chill of early March and a tea tray on the way. Roland fussed over Charlotte, placed a footstool for her, asked anxiously was she quite comfortable. Giles was restless. Walking slightly stiffly after a day in the saddle, he went over to the window and looked out into the dusk.

"I suppose it's too late to go and see Mrs. Brown today," he said regretfully.

Roland looked round. "You are excessively eager to meet the lady. A beautiful young widow, is she?" He chuckled to show he was roasting Giles.

"Quite attractive as I remember. I've only met her once."

So Cassandra Brown was young and attractive, was she? Jodie thought. Somehow she had pictured the physicist as middle-aged, dumpy, and most certainly bespectacled. Of course Giles was only keen to see her again because of her knowledge—but keen he undoubtedly was.

"How do I go about sending her a message that we would like to call tomorrow morning?" he was asking.

"Write a note and send one of the footmen with it," Charlotte advised. "Tell him to wait for an answer."

"Is nine o'clock all right, Jodie?" Giles asked.

Charlotte shook her head. "It is not proper to pay morning calls before eleven. Mrs. Brown may be dancing half the night away tonight, for all we know."

Giles looked startled at the idea. Jodie found his incredulity consoling. At least his image of Cassandra was not of a beautiful young woman enjoying the amusements of London.

A sudden thought struck Jodie. "Dancing! Charlotte, if you are to chaperone me to balls, I must learn your dances. I refuse to be a wallflower."

"Unthinkable," said Roland gallantly.

"I shall teach you," Emily promised, her brown eyes sparkling. "We shall start tomorrow. Roland, will you help me demonstrate the steps? And then partner Jodie while she practises? Oh, it will be such fun going to balls with Jodie, will it not, Charlotte?"

Charlotte agreed, unoffended by the implication that going to balls without Jodie had been less than fun. Later that evening she confided to Jodie that when they were in London in the autumn she had been too unsure of herself to give her sister-in-law the support she needed.

"Emily is right," she said. "We shall go on much better with you to show us the way. You may not be conversant with all our odd customs, but you are so—so *intrepid*."

Jodie's supply of intrepidity ran low that night. Lying wakeful in her bed, her feet on a hot brick wrapped in flannel, she felt very far from home.

She listened to the watch calling the hours, the occasional clop of hooves and rumble of wheels as a carriage passed in the street: sounds more alien than any she had heard at night at Waterstock. Besides, she had known Waterstock Manor, however briefly, in her own time. The very house itself had been a link with the future. Here in the great city Giles was more than ever her only lifeline, and Giles cared for nothing but his theories and Cassandra Brown.

Would she ever see Mom and Dad again?

Don't be silly, she told herself sharply. Feeling sorry for herself would get her nowhere. She decided to read for a while to take her mind off her worries. Dinah, who had unpacked for her, had put the biography of Ada Byron beside her bed. Now there was someone with real problems.

It was not as easy as reaching out to turn on the bedside lamp. She had blown out her candle hours ago. There was a box of lucifers on the dressing table, with the little bottle of oil of vitriol needed to ignite them. And that, according to Giles, was concentrated sulfuric acid. Not something to be messed with in the dark. Nor did she think she could strike a spark with the tinderbox in the dark.

Emily had said that a lamp was always left burning on

the landing. Shivering, Jodie slipped out of bed and felt for her slippers and wrapper. Carrying the unlit candle in its holder, she tiptoed out of her chamber. Yes, there was the lamp, turned down low, with a jar of spills beside it.

There was also a line of light under the door of Giles's chamber. Talking to Giles would be even better than reading. Jodie tapped on the door.

"Come in." His voice was tired and abstracted.

She opened the door, stepped in, closed it softly behind her. The room was chilly, the fire of banked sea-coal barely flickering. In a brown velvet dressing gown, Giles was sitting at a small table, his inevitable sheaf of papers before him. He continued to write for a moment before he looked up.

"What is it, Jodie?"

"I can't sleep. I thought we could talk for a while." She saw that his eyes were red-rimmed with fatigue. "But I won't disturb you, I'll just sit quietly. Can I get into your bed? My feet are cold."

"No, you cannot." He spoke quietly but with determination. "You must be mad. What if someone has heard you moving about, seen you come in here? I know we are supposed to be half-brother and -sister, but considering what Charles has told me of the scandal flying about his friend Byron, that would be no protection for you whatsoever."

"Charlotte and Emily would not tell tales."

"No, but it would distress them. The servants would most certainly gossip, and Roland would throw us out on our ears."

"Oh, all right." Jodie felt disconsolate but knew she sounded petulant. "What are you doing?"

"I'm *trying* to get my theories in order for Dr. Brown tomorrow."

"Damn Dr. Brown. Can't you think of anyone else?" Tears pricking her eyelids, she turned and flung out of the room, scarcely remembering to move quietly. All she wanted was a bit of comfort, and all he could think of was his damned physics. And Dr. Brown.

Determinedly she blinked the tears away and lit her candle from the lamp with a spill. More than ever she needed the distraction of a good book.

Ada Byron's life absorbed her: the bright, sickly child, growing up with only her dogs and her horse for affection; the bitter, self-righteous mother, often absent, exacting love as well as obedience from the daughter who feared her; the mysterious, never-revealed portrait of the father behind its velvet curtain, and the volumes of his poetry, proudly displayed but never to be read. Lady Byron's friends had dinned into Ada that she owed an unpayable debt to her suffering mother, that the slightest disobedience might be the cause of Annabella's death. Instead, it was her famous and infamous father who died, in exile, when Ada was eight, his last words not of the fight he had led for Greek independence but of his little daughter, long lost to him.

Then Ada at seventeen, in London for her first Season, met Charles Babbage, mathematician and brilliant inventor. Jodie fell asleep over a description of his Analytical Engine.

"Have you ever heard of Charles Babbage?" she asked Giles at breakfast, her pique long forgotten. Only Emily was present; Roland insisted that Charlotte break her fast in bed and this morning had joined her in their chamber.

"Babbage? Yes, of course. His Difference Engine is—will be in the Science Museum in Kensington, still in working order. If he'd ever completed his Analytical Engine it would have been the first real computer. Good lord, is that the Ada you keep talking about? I didn't think her name was Byron, though."

"She marries Lord Lovelace, but I haven't reached that part of the book yet."

"Ada Lovelace? That's it. There's a computer language named after her, an international standard for certain applications. She's generally regarded as the first computer programmer. She foresaw all sorts of possibilities that Babbage's mechanical machine probably would never have been able to carry out, even if he'd had the support to finish building it."

"She really was—will be brilliant then? She certainly intended to make her mark, though she wasn't sure if it would be in math or music. She wanted to equal her father's fame."

"You mean Lord Byron?" asked Emily. "He really is famous in the future?"

"For his poetry, mostly, but he's also going to inspire half of Europe to throw the Turks out of Greece," Jodie explained. "I suppose in a way it's just as well he has to leave England."

"I find it difficult to imagine him as a hero when all the world considers him a villain. It is a very odd feeling to hear all this before it happens."

Giles apologized. "It's not fair of us to talk about it in your presence. I'm amazed at how you have adjusted to our peculiar circumstances. We'd have been well and truly stuck without your help."

Jodie nodded agreement as Emily blushed. At that moment Charlotte came in, her round, pretty face blooming under a delightful bonnet of blue velvet with an artfully curled ostrich feather dyed to match.

"What, still at table? I am ready to go out. Emily, I have received a note from my sister. She is in town; do you care to go with me to see her? Jodie, Cousin Giles, we can take you up in the barouche as far as Lady Bestor's house, or Potter shall call a hackney if you prefer. Then, later this afternoon, Roland means to introduce you to his club, Giles, while we ladies make some absolutely essential purchases."

Her blue eyes sparkled at the prospect. Nor was Jodie averse to exploring the shops of the greatest city in the world. Not only was shopping fun, she pointed out to Emily as they went up to put on their bonnets, but it must surely be classified as a popular pastime, qualifying as a research topic.

"If not the most popular," Emily agreed.

Hurrying into her borrowed pelisse, Jodie ran downstairs to where Giles was waiting in the hall and whispered, "I'm sorry I was unreasonable last night."

"I'm sorry I snapped." He gave her a quick, entirely brotherly hug. "Tell me, how can I get out of going with Roland to his club this afternoon?"

Jodie considered. "It is something of an honour to be invited, I collect. Roland may be shockingly offended if you do not go, at least this once."

"You're the historian." He pulled a face. "My father put me up for the Liberal Club, but I never could stand the fusty old place."

She grinned. "If you are expecting a fusty old place, I suspect you may be pleasantly surprised."

Charlotte emerged from Roland's study and Emily pattered down the stairs. They went out to the barouche.

It was only a few blocks to Lady Bestor's address in Dover Street. Jodie drank in the sights on the way. She would persuade Giles to walk home, she decided, so as to investigate further. They drove round Berkeley Square and there was Gunter's, at the sign of the Pineapple, just as she had seen it described in a dozen books. Though the second day of March was a bit chilly for eating an ice, Jodie was determined to pay the famous confectioner a visit. All in the name of research, of course.

The barouche set them down at the door of Lady Bestor's little house. Giles knocked. Standing on the step, Jodie wondered if they were on a wild goose chase. Dr. Brown's letter had been totally noncommittal. She might not want to help—but then she need not have answered at all and they could never have found her. Perhaps she would be unable to help, another victim of an irreversible accident. Who was Lady Bestor? What was Lord Font's part in all this?

Jodie clung to Giles's arm as they waited for the front door to open.

= 7 =

A FOOTMAN OPENED the door. Giles gave their names and he and Jodie were ushered into a narrow hall, decorated on one side with a hunting tapestry and on the other with a family portrait overflowing with children.

"Her ladyship is expecting you." The footman opened another door. "Mr. and Miss Faringdale, my lady."

There were three people in the drawing room: an ancient lady, thin and twisted with rheumatism, sitting on a sofa; a tall, blond gentleman, standing by the window; and an elegant woman in her late twenties, with reddish-brown ringlets and green eyes, who stepped forward to greet them.

"Good heavens, it really is you, Dr. Faringdale." Her accent was pure New England. "Or is it 'my lord?'" She stopped in confusion.

"Plain mister here, Dr. Brown—Mrs. Brown. Or better just Giles. This is . . . my half-sister, Judith."

Jodie stared, also confused, then dropped a hurried curtsy. There was a moment of silence.

"Well?" said the old lady.

Mrs. Brown started. "Allow me to present you to Lady Bestor. And this is Harry—Lord Font."

The tall gentleman bowed. Jodie curtsied again, feeling increasingly silly, then turned back to Mrs. Brown.

"You're Cassandra? The physicist? Excuse me, it's ridiculous but I pictured you in a white coat like scientists wear on . . . Oh!" She glanced in alarm at the other two strangers.

The old crone winked at her. "Not to worry, missie, I know all there is to know." Her sharp eyes turned to Lord

Font. "Or all I need to know, at least. Well, Harry, now I've satisfied my curiosity I'll leave you in peace." She reached for her cane. "Help me up."

Lord Font reached her in one long stride, and laid his hand on her frail shoulder. "Do not stir, Aunt Tavie. We shall entertain our guests in the dining parlour. Please come this way, Miss Judith, Mr. Faringdale."

We, Jodie noted, following him, *our* guests. And that was a monstrous intimate look he gave Mrs. Brown as he seated her at the long oak table.

She was beautiful. God send she was spoken for.

They exchanged stories. Mrs. Brown had also come to the past by accident. With the aid of her calculator and a competent assistant in Lord Font, she had returned home before deciding that the nineteenth century was more to her taste.

Giles sat back with a sigh of relief. "You have a calculator, then, and the calculations already done. All we have to do is plug in the figures for a slightly different time and place."

Mrs. Brown and Lord Font exchanged glances. "I fear not," said the latter. "Cassandra destroyed everything."

In the deathly hush, the cry of a hawker in the street was plain: "Hot, hot, hot—pudding hot!"

"The Flying Pieman," said Lord Font irrelevantly.

At any other time Jodie would have been intrigued. Now all she could do was say in horrified tones, "Destroyed? Everything? But why?"

Mrs. Brown shrugged her shoulders. "Harry hasn't much faith in the law of Conservation of Reality. We were afraid they might be found and used to alter the timestream."

"I have to agree with Lord Font," Giles said unwillingly. "I'm sorry, Dr. Brown, but I just don't think it can account for more than minor changes. It's our bad luck that we arrived after you got rid of the calculator. Still, at least you have a theory that you know works. I take it you are willing to help us?"

"Of course," came instant affirmation from both.

At once Giles became businesslike. He untied the roll of papers he had set before him on the table and shuffled through them. "I have drawn up designs for a slide rule cursor. If we can have it made, it will greatly help in redoing your calculations. I'd like you to check my drawings."

"I don't know anything about slide rules," Mrs. Brown confessed. "I was brought up with calculators. But Harry used his slide rule to check all my figures."

Lord Font pulled Giles's papers towards him as Giles grinned crookedly at Jodie and said, "You see the advantages of an old-fashioned education."

That was the last notice anyone took of her. Lord Font went to fetch his slide rule, and the two twentieth-century physicists began a discussion of twentieth-century physics that might as well have been in Greek for all Jodie understood. In fact, some of it seemed to be in Greek. She heard talk of tau-space and epsilon-something-else and when they spoke of pi it was not the Flying Pieman they meant.

Pi r squared, thought Jodie idly. The circumference of a circle. No, probably the area. It was as bad as volts and watts and ohms, which they seemed to have moved on to now.

"Oh'm goin' 'ohm," she said experimentally.

"See you later," said Giles. "But look, Cassandra, if you consider . . ."

Jodie did not stay for the end of his sentence. She found a certain satisfaction in flouncing from the room. You couldn't flounce in pants.

The footman brought her pelisse, a dark-chocolate velvet coat lined with white sarsnet and luxuriously trimmed with ermine. Like her gown, also borrowed from Emily, it fitted close over the bodice then fell from a high waist to her ankles. Her feet were snug in her own boots, bought two hundred years hence with English weather in mind. To hell with Giles. It would be better on her own because she could stop and look at anything that caught her eye.

"The gentleman . . . ?" suggested the footman with an anxious air.

"He will be here for some time yet."

"A hackney, madam?"

"No, I shall walk, thank you."

Shrugging, the man opened the door for her.

Jodie set off in a mood of thorough disgruntlement. How could she have been so stupid as to suppose that Giles would not be attracted to that woman only because he did not picture her dancing the night away? She was beautiful, to be sure, but it was her mind he admired. She was a colleague, his equal in the esoteric realms of subatomic particles where the music of the spheres played for dancing quarks and neutrinos.

Pleased with the image, Jodie began to take an interest in her surroundings. This was her field of expertise, and when she reached home again she would be an unequalled expert on daily life in the Regency period.

She beamed at a passing couple. The gentleman smiled back; his companion scowled and hurried him onward.

Left on Hay Hill, a short block then right on Berkeley Street, and Berkeley Square lay ahead. Jodie had noted their route carefully.

The traffic in the square had increased considerably since they passed through in the barouche an hour ago. Gunter's was a-bustle, with waiters running to carry orders to carriages parked under the leafless trees of the central garden. The original fast food drive-in, Jodie thought with a grin.

A young man in a tight-waisted coat with hugely padded shoulders returned her grin. Doffing his glossy beaver, he bowed as far as his dangerously high shirt points allowed.

"Buy you an ice, miss?" he enquired.

Jodie was tempted. What harm could she come to in this busy place in broad daylight? Then she realized that all the women in sight were studiously avoiding looking at her, while several men, on the contrary, were looking only too hard—the sort of look that moved from face to feet and back again, pausing en route.

"Or perhaps a drop of something stronger?" her accoster suggested insinuatingly.

Hot-faced, she brushed past him and hurried on, narrowly avoiding a dashing tilbury that swept out of Bruton Street. Perhaps this had not been such a great idea after all. Come to think of it, young ladies in Regency romances were forever being told not to walk alone in London.

The wretch had taken her for a lightskirt. No, she needed stronger language than that: the son-of-a-bitch had taken her for a whore.

She was slightly out of breath when she turned the corner from Davies Street into Grosvenor Street. There was a high perch phaeton outside the Faringdales' house, the horses' heads held by a small boy in livery, and a tall gentleman was just turning away from the door. As he strode down the steps, she recognized Lord Thorncrest.

"My lord," she called, hurrying. "Thorncrest, wait!"

He swung round, frowning, but his face cleared when he saw her. "Ah, the little American. Good day, Miss Judith."

"Good day. I'm sorry, I daresay I ought not to have shouted to you like that."

He was amused. "To be sure, I am not accustomed to being accosted by females in the street—at least not in this neighbourhood. However, I shan't complain since otherwise I might have missed you, which would have been a devastating blow." He glanced beyond her. "You seem to have mislaid your companion, ma'am."

"I am alone." Jodie was annoyed to feel herself flushing again.

"Indeed." The black eyebrows rose. "American customs are very different from our own."

"Perhaps our streets are safer for unaccompanied females," she retorted.

"In that case I must infer that America boasts few females as captivating as Miss Judith Faringdale."

"From which *I* infer that England boasts many."

The earl laughed. "That was ill considered," he acknowledged. "True, beauties we have aplenty, yet to find such wit and spirit united with charm and loveliness is rare indeed."

"Then doubtless you will be glad of the opportunity to study the phenomenon further. Will you take me to see the sights of London, Thorncrest?"

"I never drive females."

Jodie sighed. "What a pity. I shall have to summon a hackney." She stepped back, looked around, and was raising her arm to wave to a passing hackney-driver when Lord Thorncrest caught her hand.

"Very well, you abominable girl. In view of the fact that we shall soon be related by marriage, I surrender. Where do you want to go?" He helped her climb up into the high carriage. His tiger jumped on behind and they started off.

"I want to see everything Londoners do for amusement."

"Everything, Miss Judith?" he drawled, his dark eyes challenging her.

Jodie refused to be cowed. "Everything," she said firmly, hoping she was not letting herself in for more than she bargained for. Emily had said his lordship was a confirmed rake. . . .

"Where is Miss Faringdale?" asked Lord Font, returning to the dining room with his slide rule.

Giles and Cassandra looked at him, then at each other.

"I think she said she was going home," Giles admitted sheepishly. "I wasn't really listening."

"Did she take a hackney? Did Culpepper go with her?"

"Culpepper?"

"Aunt Tavie's abigail," Cassandra explained. "I don't know, Harry. I didn't think anything of it."

"It's only a few blocks. Jodie's no wilting violet."

" 'Tis scarcely proper, however, for a young lady to walk alone."

"If she chooses to, there's not much I can do about it," said Giles.

"Are you not her brother?"

"As a matter of fact, no. We only met the day all this started."

Lord Font looked shocked. "It is not my place to find fault," he said stiffly.

"Don't be a fussbudget, Harry," Cassandra admonished him. "Jodie's a twentieth-century American, not a delicate young lady."

"It's not actually dangerous for her to be walking alone, is it?" Giles was beginning to worry.

"Probably not," the baron conceded, "in broad daylight

in this part of town."

"As long as she doesn't wander off to do her research. She's a historian, you know, and this happens to be her period. Perhaps I ought to go after her."

"If she didn't go straight home, you won't know where to look anyway," Cassandra pointed out impatiently. "Can we get on with figuring out how to approach these calculations?"

Giles took notes while she explained how she had worked out the details of her return to her own time. It was going to be a long job without a calculator, especially as he and Jodie would be going from a different place, with different equipment at the other end.

"Would it not be easier just to go from Font Hall?" asked Harry.

Cassandra laughed. "Dr. Jenkins would have a fit if two total strangers suddenly appeared in his lab. If you don't arrive during working hours, you will find yourselves locked in, waiting to be found in the morning. No, we'll try it from Waterstock first. Harry, how soon do you think your instrument maker can get the new and improved slide rule made?"

"That depends on how much we can pay him."

Harry and Cassandra both looked questioningly at Giles, who suddenly realized that Lord Font was not dressed in the height of fashion but on the contrary looked somewhat shabby.

"The present Lord Faringdale is rather flattered to have a man of science in the family," he said, "and is inclined to be generous. Since Charlotte—Lady Faringdale—pointed out that in effect I'm drawing on my own inheritance, I haven't scrupled to take advantage of his willingness to pay our way. Tell your man to give the cursor top priority. Conservation of Reality or no, the sooner I get Jodie away from this place, the better."

Harry Font glanced at Cassandra and laughed. "I know what you mean," he agreed.

Walking home, Giles watched as carefully for any sign of Jodie as he ever had for an anomaly in a computer graph of the accelerator. He felt guilty for letting her go alone, for not following as soon as he realized the impropriety. Still, he thought with annoyance, she was the historian, she ought to have known better. She must learn that the independent spirit which was admirable at home might prove hazardous here.

He had better deliver a warning as soon as he reached the house. The prospect made him groan. She was not likely to take kindly to the lecture.

"Is anyone in the library?" he asked Frederick as he took off his top coat. "Please tell Miss Judith I should like to see her there at once."

"The book room we calls it here, sir, it being smaller than the one at Waterstock." The footman took his coat. "I don't think as Miss Judith's come in yet. My lady and Miss Emily's waiting for her to go shopping. And his lordship said to tell you he's ready to be off to White's soon as you wants."

"Jodie's not home yet? Hell and damnation. Where is everyone?"

"In the back parlour, sir."

Giles strode down the hall to the parlour. Charlotte and Emily were busy at their needlework, while Roland thumbed impatiently through a copy of *Blackwood's Magazine*.

"Disgraceful!" he muttered. "Oh there you are, Giles. I vow I do not know what the world is coming to when they allow such things to be published."

"I am glad you are come," Charlotte welcomed him, laying aside her embroidery with a placid air. "Emily and I are longing to show dear Jodie the shops."

"Jodie isn't with me," said Giles, his voice harsh with worry. "She set out alone before me and I gather she's not home yet."

"Oh dear," said Charlotte faintly. "Wherever can she be?"

= 8 =

"THANK YOU, MY LORD, I have had a simply splendid time."
Jodie smiled up at Lord Thorncrest, very much aware that
he had not released her hand after helping her down from
the phaeton.

"It has been my pleasure, Miss Judith. I assure you, I have
seen more of London this day than in my entire life."

"More of the unexceptionable side of London perhaps. I
hope it was not too shockingly dull for a Nonpareil like
yourself."

"On the contrary, ma'am. If everyone could see the British
Museum in such enlivening company, there would be no
getting near the place."

"Well, you were unexpectedly knowledgeable company."

"I am not entirely given over to sporting pursuits. I fear
you think me a sad rattle, but I have been known to open
a book on occasion."

"I expect you read Lord Byron's poetry. You are a friend
of his, I collect. I wish you will introduce me to him."

He looked at her oddly. "Perhaps."

Jodie remembered that the poet was in utter disgrace at
present, and somewhat disreputable at the best of times,
no fit acquaintance for a respectable young lady. "Will you
come in for some refreshment?" she asked hurriedly. "I
expect Charlotte and Emily are home by now."

He drew a gold watch from his fob pocket and opened it.
"Pray make my excuses, I am expected elsewhere. I shall
call on the morrow and hope to find the ladies at home."

Escorting her to the door, he knocked, then raised his hat

and bowed over her hand. She felt the pressure of his lips through her glove.

Surely the custom of kissing a lady's hand was obsolete by now, she thought. A gentleman was supposed to make only a token gesture in that direction. However, she was not about to object to the real thing from so handsome a gentleman as Lord Thorncrest. It was not as if Emily cared for him.

As the door opened she smiled at him again. "Good day, my lord, and once more thank you."

He nodded, touched his hat in salute, and ran down the steps, his elegant clothes unable to conceal the powerful vigor of every motion. Jodie recalled a phrase from some Regency she had read: "he strips to advantage." She was prepared to wager that the earl stripped to advantage.

Potter's shocked face brought her back to earth. He couldn't have read her mind!

"Miss Judith, everyone's in such a worry."

"Oh dear." She was instantly contrite. "I ought to have left a message. It never crossed my mind that they might wonder where I was."

The butler's seamed face softened. "Never you mind, miss. All's well that ends well, though I don't doubt there'll be a peal rung over you. The family's in the back parlour."

Jodie trod down the hall with considerable trepidation. If Roland treated her like an incompetent child, she was not sure whether she'd be able to hold her tongue. She and Giles were greatly indebted to the viscount and would find it difficult to manage without his support, but there were limits to her patience.

She was not prepared for Charlotte bursting into tears at the sight of her.

Emily ran up and hugged her. "Dearest Jodie, we have been quite anxious about you." She added in a whisper, "*I* knew you were all right. Roland is in a fearful pelter, and poor Giles blames himself for letting you go off alone."

A glance at Roland's expression confirmed that diagnosis, but Giles's thundercloud face suggested that to his mind the blame was all Jodie's.

"Lord Thorncrest was kind enough to drive me about to

69

see the sights," she said defensively. "I am sorry you were all set at sixes and sevens, but I was perfectly safe." She suppressed the memory of the "gentleman" who had accosted her in Berkeley Square.

"Lord Thorncrest!" Roland exploded. "Why, the man is a confirmed . . ."

"That's enough, dear," said Charlotte with resolution, her tears wiped away and forgotten. "I believe Cousin Giles wishes to speak to Jodie. Come, Emily." She took Roland's arm and practically dragged him from the room, pausing only to kiss Jodie's cheek on the way. Emily followed, her backward glance commiserating.

"I had a delightful time." Jodie drew off her gloves with a nervous movement, avoiding Giles's eye. "Thorncrest took me to see a panorama of the battle of Waterloo, and the British Museum, and several other places. I must make notes while I remember everything."

"I suppose you know what Roland was about to say." Giles's voice was ominously quiet. "The earl is a notorious womanizer, a playboy, a rakehell in this era's parlance."

"Then Roland has no business wedding his sister to him!" Jodie flared.

"You know better than that. Sit down, Jodie." His grip was iron on her arm. She was glad to escape into a chair by the fire. Chilled, she held out her hands to the flames.

Giles remained standing, scowling down at her. "Marriage in this age has nothing to do with a man's virtue, or lack thereof, and everything to do with a woman's. As a historian, you should know that better than I. It was bad enough that you walked through the streets alone. . . ."

"I told you I was leaving."

A tinge of colour crept into his cheeks, but he continued grimly, "I am at fault too, but I am not your keeper and as I said, you are the historian. You must have been aware that it was unwise, to say the least. And then to go out driving unchaperoned with a notorious rake!"

"He was charming. And besides, his tiger was with us."

"Tiger?" Giles was momentarily diverted by the image this conjured up.

"A small boy in livery who hangs on behind."

"You see, you know more of this period than I shall ever know, God willing." He ran his fingers through his hair. "Jodie, you *must* have a care for your reputation."

Surging to her feet, she snapped her fingers under his nose. "I don't give that for my reputation. For crying out loud, Giles, I don't belong in this time, I don't intend to marry here, I lost my virginity long ago, and you are not my guardian."

"Precisely what I told Harry Font." He grinned wryly as she glared at him in outrage, hands on hips. "No, not about your virginity. But you see, that's just the point; you wouldn't want him to know that." He slumped wearily into a chair. "You lose your precious reputation and Roland's not going to want you hanging around his virtuous wife and sister. If he throws us out we're in serious trouble. We're going to be here for a while, maybe a long while."

"How long?" She dropped to her knees beside his chair. "How long? Do you mean we might be stuck for ever?"

"I don't know. I wish to hell Cassandra hadn't destroyed her calculator. With just the slide rule it's going to be hit or miss at best."

Jodie felt the blood drain from her face. "You mean it? We might be stuck here? But my family!" she cried in anguish.

"And mine," he said sombrely, taking her hands in his warm, strong clasp. "Perhaps I shouldn't have told you."

"I'm an adult." She gazed up, reading his eyes. "I know you will do everything that can be done to get us home. I trust you, Giles, now and always."

His look changed. He put one hand to her face, caressing her cheek, and leaned towards her for a breathless moment. Then he flung out of the chair, almost knocking her over.

"You're my sister."

"*One*, two, three. *One*, two, three," counted Charlotte. "That is very good, Jodie. Pray play a little faster, Emily."

The lilting waltz tune quickened and Roland propelled Jodie round the drawing room, its carpet rolled back for the lesson. He was not a bad dancer, though his face was growing somewhat red after two country dances and a cotillion. He appeared to be enjoying himself.

The door opened.

"Lord Thorncrest is come, my lady," announced Potter. "Are you at home?"

With a doubtful glance at Jodie, Charlotte hesitated.

"Yes, yes, show him in," Roland said, yesterday's condemnation of the earl forgotten or dismissed. His feathers were easily ruffled, but as easily smoothed. He pulled out a huge white muslin handkerchief and blotted his forehead. "How d'ye do, Thorncrest. Just teaching my cousin a few of our English dances."

The earl stood in the doorway, regarding the scene with his usual sardonic look. "Perhaps I might be allowed to take over your duties for a while, Faringdale. May I have this dance, Miss Judith?"

"Thank you, my lord," said Jodie demurely, "but I believe I shall do better to stay with the teacher to whom I am accustomed."

Roland nodded his approval. "You could stand up with Emily, Thorncrest," he suggested. "Charlotte, my dear, you will not mind a turn at the pianoforte?"

Charlotte took Emily's place at the keyboard. A less accomplished pianist than Emily, she began to play with strongly marked time as if she was still counting her "*one*, two, three." Emily curtsied to Thorncrest, who bowed, took her hand, and led her onto the floor.

"I should like to watch for a minute," Jodie said. She and Roland stepped back out of the way.

Emily moved stiffly in her partner's arms, her eyes focused on his waistcoat buttons. He said something, and her gaze moved up as far as his cravat, a miracle of starched muslin creased in intricate folds. Again he spoke. She looked up into his face and began to answer as they swung towards Jodie and Roland.

". . . said you promised to take her on a steam packet on the Thames."

"I hope you will go. . . ."

They danced away, Emily relaxed now, gliding smoothly across the floor as if her toes were an inch above the surface. She and the earl were both excellent dancers, a pleasure to watch together. Jodie recognized that Emily responded pliantly to Thorncrest's slightest lead, so that they moved as one.

Unable to give up her autonomy, even for the sake of a dance, Jodie would never dance as well. It was fun, though. She tugged Roland back onto the floor.

The waltz thumped to its end. Roland whipped out his handkerchief again.

"Excellent, Cousin, excellent, but enough for today, I think. I shall be happy to stand up with you at your first ball."

"We already have an invitation to a ball," Charlotte told Lord Thorncrest, "though the Season is scarcely begun."

"Whose ball is that, ma'am? I hope I have not already thrown away my invitation."

Jodie was unable to suppress an unladylike snort at the implications of this speech. Plainly the earl was certain he had received an invitation, whoever the hostess was, and equally plainly he was in the habit of discarding invitations unanswered. Charlotte, however, understood only that his lordship intended to change his mind about attending the event on hearing that the Faringdales were to be present.

"Lady Cowper's ball," she informed him, beaming. "It is some ten days hence."

"Ah yes, the estimable Lady Cowper," he murmured, then said to Charlotte with his charming smile, "May I hope to lead you out for a quadrille, ma'am?"

"Oh, I do not think . . ." Charlotte glanced anxiously at Roland. "I shall be chaperoning. . . ."

"But I insist. What are we bachelors to do if the pretty young matrons abandon the floor? I shall count on it." Leaving her in blushing confusion, he turned to Emily with smooth politeness. "You will reserve a waltz and supper for me, Miss Emily? Thank you, I am honoured. Oh, and Miss Judith," he added, as if in an afterthought. "A country dance, perhaps?"

"Perhaps," Jodie agreed pertly, sure that he was teasing her.

He laughed. "To return to the present, since the sky has cleared Miss Emily has accepted my invitation to drive in the park, if we may have your kind permission, Lady Faringdale."

He had told Jodie he never drove females! She suspected he was well aware that he had set the household by the ears when he took her out yesterday. He was not averse to causing trouble, but at least he seemed to be making some small effort to atone—if only to tease her further, she realized as she caught his mocking glance.

Roland invited Jodie and Charlotte to accompany him to the park in the barouche. The ladies went upstairs to put on their bonnets and pelisses.

Charlotte begged Jodie to come into her dressing room for a moment. "What am I to do?" she wailed. "I could not refuse Lord Thorncrest but Roland has forbidden me to dance."

"Because he thinks you are pregnant? What a knuckle-head. Don't worry about it, for heaven's sake, Charlotte. The ball is ten days away; by then you will probably have seen the doctor and told Roland you were mistaken."

"I have already made an appointment." She looked guilty. "I wanted to put it off as long as possible so it is not for two weeks, after the ball. But I *like* dancing. I *want* to dance."

"There's no earthly reason you shouldn't, even if you really were pregnant. Tell me, has Roland stopped making . . . um . . . insisting on his conjugal rights?"

Charlotte crimsoned to the roots of her blonde curls. "You mean, because I am breeding?" she whispered, glancing nervously at the door. "He offered to, but I told him—Oh Jodie, I cannot talk about it." She hid her face in her hands.

"No, I'm sorry, I should not have asked." Jodie paused. "All the same, you just be brave and tell him that if you can do *that*, you can dance."

Unexpectedly, Charlotte giggled, then bit her lip. "I shall try," she promised.

Emily, already dressed to go out with Lord Thorncrest,

was waiting in Jodie's chamber.

"What shall I say to him?" she wailed. "I shall be all alone with him for at least an hour."

"You managed very well while you were dancing." Jodie took her pelisse from the wardrobe and sat down at the dressing table to tidy her hair before putting on her hat.

"That was because I know how much you want to go to the Tower, and Astley's, and on the river. Roland will probably hint him away from inviting you, but I thought if I told Lord Thorncrest *I* want to see all those things, he would have to ask me too, and Roland could not possibly object. And it worked. We are to go on the steam packet to Richmond on the first convenient fine day."

Jodie hugged her. "What a darling you are, Emily. Tell me, do you think steam will ever replace sails as a way of crossing the oceans?"

"The engines would have to be very much improved. I read an article . . . Oh Jodie, you already know the answer!"

"Yes, but Thorncrest does not. Ask him his opinion."

"I doubt he has one."

"You cannot know until you ask," Jodie pointed out. "Besides, I believe he is more intelligent than he chooses to appear. I told you he knew what he was talking about at the museum yesterday. Anyway, that does not matter. If he has no opinion, then tell him yours. Just try to pretend that he's a normal person."

Emily went off into whoops. "A normal person!" she gasped. "Neither abnormal nor subnormal? Oh dear, I wish you had not said that. I shall not be able to look at him without laughing."

"And a very good thing too," said Jodie, tying the ribbons of her hat firmly beneath her chin.

= 9 =

GILES WAS SPENDING by far too much of his time at Lady
Bestor's house. Jodie was not jealous, she assured herself,
especially since it turned out that Cassandra was engaged
to Harry Font. But it was not healthy for Giles to concentrate on his calculations to the exclusion of all else. Every
morning he went to Dover Street, and whether he returned
for luncheon or not till dinner, he spent the rest of the day
and evening in the book room, with his papers and his
modernized slide rule.

He needed a break.

On the other hand, Jodie had been reading how Ada
Lovelace's scientific career was, or rather would be, cut
short by interruptions. Family duties, illness, her mother's
bizarre behaviour, and finally a passion for gambling would
distract her from her work after the one brilliant paper.
Jodie had no desire to figure in future history as the cause
of Giles's failure to reach his full potential.

Roland rescued her from the dilemma by insisting that
Giles must attend Lady Cowper's ball.

Charlotte seconded him. "Since we called on Lady Cowper, she has kindly sent another invitation specifically
addressed to you and Jodie. It will not do to offend her,
Cousin Giles. She is one of the patronesses of Almack's and
though she is prodigious good-humoured you will not want
to risk Jodie not receiving vouchers."

"I won't?" said Giles blankly. "What's Almack's?"

Emily hastened to explain. "It is a club where the most
exclusive dancing assemblies are held every Wednesday

during the Season. For a young lady, not to receive vouchers is to be banished to the outskirts of Society."

"Heaven forbid that any act of mine should banish Jodie to the outskirts of Society." Giles grinned. "All right, I'll go to this ball of yours."

"A noble sacrifice, dear Giles," said Jodie.

That very evening he abandoned his calculations to go with them to a concert of the Philharmonic Society in Hanover Square. It was one of the items on Jodie's list of "Things to do in Town," much of it culled from the latest edition of the *Picture of London*.

Jodie managed to cram several amusements into each day, from Bullock's Museum and Mrs. Salmon's Waxwork to a balloon ascension and afternoon tea with the Duchess of Richmond. For all her bashfulness, young Lady Faringdale moved in the first circles. Though the Season was scarce begun, Charlotte had obtained invitations to a rout, a ridotto, an informal hop, a Venetian breakfast and a card party (Jodie had strict instructions from Roland not to introduce pinochle). They had been to Drury Lane to see Edmund Kean, and to Gunter's for ices. Jodie's reams of notes were piled as high as Giles's.

That was most satisfactory, but still more pleasing was the change in Emily and Charlotte. Encouraged by Jodie's total lack of shyness, they blossomed in her company. After one short week, Emily had two youthful admirers and Roland was so swelled with pride in his wife that Jodie kept watching for his waistcoat buttons to pop off.

"I am hardly afraid of Lord Thorncrest at all," Emily confided to Jodie as they went up to dress for Lady Cowper's ball. "To think that only a week since I dreaded the prospect of taking supper with him tonight! Now I know that if I ask his opinion of something I have read, he will converse perfectly intelligently, without the least sarcasm."

"I am waiting for the moment when he asks *your* opinion. All men appreciate a willing listener, but he is not yet aware of you as an intelligent person in your own right."

"He is aware of you, I think."

"As an individual, yes." Jodie laughed. "Intelligent I'm

not so sure of. Amusing and infuriating perhaps."

He could hardly fail to be aware of Emily's beauty tonight, Jodie thought as they descended the stairs, arms about each other's waists, some time later. White was *de rigueur* for a young lady in her first Season, but Charlotte, with an unerring eye, had compromised. Emily's gown consisted of a daffodil satin slip worn under a frothy frock of white net. The overall effect emphasized Emily's creamy skin tones, exposed by the low neckline and tiny puff sleeves. Anticipation had brought a becoming colour to her cheeks.

Jodie was quite pleased with her own appearance too. With Charlotte's concurrence, she had chosen a gown of amber silk, trimmed with old ivory lace. It flattered the unfashionable tan that gave credence to Charlotte's oft-whispered explanation of her "Red Indian" ancestry. Dinah had long since given up her efforts with the curling tongs and instead had woven a borrowed strand of amber beads through the black coils of Jodie's hair.

Charlotte, in blue, having overseen the last details of their toilettes, led them down the stairs and into the drawing room where the gentlemen awaited their appearance.

Lord Thorncrest's eyes widened when he caught sight of Emily. However, his expression held as much smugness as admiration, and his words conveyed as much self-satisfaction as compliment.

"I see I am to be congratulated on having chosen a diamond of the first water."

Jodie almost forgave him when he presented her with a nosegay of yellow rosebuds. He had obviously gone to the trouble of enquiring about their gowns, since Emily's posy was also yellow and Charlotte's white.

Giles was beside her, elegant in black coat and satin knee-breeches.

"Beautiful," he murmured. "But then I thought you beautiful in denim jeans."

Jodie found herself blushing like the veriest ninnyhammer, especially when she remembered that he had also seen her in far less, back in the Waterstock stables.

She thoroughly enjoyed the ball, just the sort of glittering affair she had so often read about. Their hostess greeted them graciously, and Charlotte pointed out several notables Jodie had read of. Among these was a handsome, red-headed gentleman she named as Lord Palmerston.

On seeing him, Jodie plucked at Giles's sleeve. "Lady Cowper's his mistress," she whispered, "or at least they're very good friends. Her mother, Lady Melbourne, on her deathbed tells Emily to be true to him and she'll marry him eventually, when she's widowed and he's prime minister."

"Scandalmonger," said Giles, amused.

"How many people have a chance to tattle about the future as well as the present? Lady Melbourne herself had any number of lovers. In fact the future Lord Melbourne, who will be prime minister too, is supposed to be Lord Egremont's son. He's married to Caro Lamb, the one who fooled around with Byron."

"I've heard of her. She was mad, wasn't she?"

"Definitely peculiar. She sent Byron clippings of her pubic hair, among other escapades."

"Good heavens!"

"*Glenarvon,* her *roman à clef,* will come out this year," Jodie went on. "It savages both Byron and Lady Melbourne who, by the way, are also 'very good friends' though she's so much older. And Lord Melbourne is Lady Byron's cousin, into the bargain. I wonder if Byron is here?" She stood on tiptoe and peered around the crowded ballroom. "Talk about an incestuous society. I'm amazed they care two hoots about poor Augusta Leigh."

"Augusta Leigh?"

"Byron's half-sister, that he had an affair with. No doubt you'll be hearing all that gossip as you're not an innocent young lady and you won't be dancing."

"On the contrary. I mean, yes I have already heard that scandal, and no I'm not an innocent young lady, but I shall be dancing. I hope you will waltz with me?"

"You took lessons on the sly," she accused.

"No, it's just another advantage of an old-fashioned education."

She smiled, glad that Cassandra had not taught him, and allowed him to swirl her about the floor with unexpected abandon.

Emily was much in demand, not sitting out a single dance, and Thorncrest watched her with a possessive air. Though their betrothal had not been announced, rumours were circulating. Jodie heard more than one matron enviously congratulate Charlotte on her sister-in-law's splendid catch. The earl had evaded the matchmaking mamas for years.

His complacency did not stop him flirting abominably with Jodie when they stood up together.

Charlotte herself danced once with the earl, once with her husband and once with Giles. Then Roland insisted on her taking her place with the chaperones, where she sat looking a little forlorn. Jodie made a point of returning to her after every set.

"It is our fault, Giles's and mine, that Roland thinks you are breeding," she whispered remorsefully.

"Oh no, you must not blame yourself. It was entirely my idea to make such a fuss about the nursery." She brightened. "I shall see Dr. Croft the day after tomorrow, so I shall be able to dance as much as I wish at the next ball."

Roland wanted to leave early, but Charlotte refused to spoil Emily's and Jodie's enjoyment. The sky was already paling in the east when they drove home after the ball. It seemed to Jodie a bit silly to go to bed. Hyped up, as she put it, she was ready to start a new day. Roland persuaded her that it was simply not done; a lady was supposed to lie abed until noon on the morning after a ball.

The morning after that, however, the entire household was astir betimes. Everyone from the viscount to the lowliest scullery maid knew that Dr. Croft was expected—and why.

Charlotte was in a flutter. She scandalized Roland by asking Jodie to be present during the doctor's examination.

"Cousin Judith is unmarried," he pointed out.

"Yes, but she is older than I and—and besides, Red Indians understand these things," Charlotte invented wildly, her bottom lip quivering and tears swimming in her blue eyes.

Her husband was not proof against this appeal. "I thought you had asked your sister to come," he said plaintively. "Since you did not—if Cousin Judith does not object?"

"Not at all." Jodie was more than willing to lend Charlotte her support. Besides, after reading about the incompetent doctors who mistreated Ada Byron's various illnesses with vast quantities of laudanum, she was both curious and anxious to add a note of sanity to the proceedings if necessary.

Dr. Richard Croft, the eminent accoucheur, had a bedside manner that explained his popularity with the ladies of Society, guaranteed to put the most nervous patient at ease. What the world had gained in medicine by the end of the twentieth century, Jodie reflected, it had lost in kindliness. The doctor put a number of questions to Charlotte in a paternal tone, and by the time he asked if she would object to removing the upper part of her clothing, she was quite composed.

She clung to Jodie's hand while Dr. Croft gently examined her breasts. Jodie expected him to do a pelvic exam, but never having been pregnant herself she was not sure if it was necessary, so did not make an issue of it. Besides, the notion might have sent Charlotte into hysterics.

"My lady," he said with a smile, "I am happy to inform you that you are approximately six weeks pregnant."

Charlotte gaped at him. "But I cannot be! I mean, I . . . the . . ."

"Her period," Jodie came to the rescue. "Menstruation."

"The menses do occasionally continue for a month or two after conception. You mentioned, ma'am, that it was a light flow. It is nothing to be concerned about, though I advise you to avoid exertion for the next two or three weeks. If the bleeding should recur, call me in. Otherwise, you are a healthy young woman, I foresee no difficulties. No horseback riding, if you please, and limit yourself to two or three dances at a ball. I shall be happy to attend your lying-in if you wish, but any competent midwife should do as well.

Good day, ma'am." With a bow to Charlotte and a nod for Jodie, the doctor departed.

Jodie and Charlotte looked at each other.

"Roland was right after all." Charlotte giggled.

"In every way," Jodie agreed, grinning.

They both collapsed in gales of mirth.

In the midst of her laughter, Jodie recalled what she had read about Dr. Richard Croft—or rather, Sir Richard Croft. It must be the same man; doubtless he would soon be knighted or inherit a baronetcy. Next year he would be Princess Charlotte's obstetrician. The heir to the throne would die in childbirth, and the doctor, blamed by the public though not by the royal family, would commit suicide a few months later.

Reminded of the primitive state of medicine, Jodie sobered. There was no guarantee that kind, practical Charlotte was to be the mother of the next Viscount Faringdale, even though Roland was Giles's ancestor. If she suffered her royal namesake's fate, Roland would simply marry again and have children by his second wife.

Charlotte had stopped laughing and was looking questioningly at Jodie. Fortunately at that moment Roland and Emily came in, saving Jodie from the need to explain her sudden gravity.

A partial knowledge of the future was definitely a mixed blessing.

Later that day, vouchers arrived from Lady Cowper for the Almack's assembly the following week. Jodie had passed the test and been judged unexceptionable.

"But *not* unexceptional," Emily teased her. "No one could possibly be more exceptional than you are."

Charlotte readily promised Roland that she would not dance at Almack's, nor at Mrs. Carpenter's ball two days later. Since discovering that she really was pregnant, she had attained a serenity that Jodie admired and envied. She accepted Roland's sometimes irritating solicitude with a patient good-humour much better suited to her character than the guilt she had felt before. Nor did she repine at being unable to dance; the baby was far too precious to risk.

* * *

To Jodie, Almack's was an illustration come to life. All that she had read about it, the pictures she had seen, were suddenly infused with light and sound and movement.

In the receiving line, Mrs. Drummond-Burrell nodded haughtily while next to her Lady Jersey, popularly known as Silence, chattered with the expected vivacity. Gentlemen in knee-breeches and ringletted ladies hopped and skipped their way through a country dance to a lively tune from the musicians in the gallery above. The odour of wax candles burning in the great chandeliers vied with a hundred expensive perfumes.

And it was hot. After a couple of sets, Jodie was glad to retreat to the less crowded supper room with Lord Thorncrest, though the refreshments were notoriously stingy.

"What do you think of Society's Mecca, Miss Judith?" he enquired, presenting her with a glass of orgeat. "You have nothing similar in America, I daresay?"

She sipped cautiously at the sweet drink. "I believe New York society is very exclusive." She was getting good at avoiding questions about her homeland. "It is interesting, but on the whole I prefer a private ball or even an informal dance. I keep feeling Countess Lieven's eyes on me, waiting for me to do something wrong and damn myself forever."

The earl's eyebrow quirked at her use of a word reserved for masculine lips but he said only, "Very true. An informal gathering of friends must certainly be preferable to a crowd of strangers of who-knows-what provenance." He gazed about the room with a look of disdain that deserved a quizzing glass, then his face brightened as two plainly but perfectly-clad gentlemen came through from the ballroom. "Ah, there are George and Scrope. May I present Mr. Brummel and Mr. Davies to you, Miss Judith?"

Fascinated, she nodded her assent and he waved to the pair. Beau Brummel and Scrope Berdmore Davies, the founder of the dandy set and one of its leaders. What a scoop!

Brummel looked unwell, and his legendary witty repartee was sadly lacking. Jodie remembered, pityingly, that he was deep in the River Tick and in a month or two would flee to France, pursued by creditors. Davies had a similar fate in store some years hence. In the meantime, as one of Byron's closest friends, he would accompany the poet to Dover on his way into exile.

How many others of the bright, laughing company were living on borrowed time? How many were living by their wits, like Brummel and Davies, or gambling away inherited fortunes; how many were persuing rich husbands for aristocratic but impoverished maidens, or rich wives to keep younger sons from debtors' prison; and how many, like Roland and Thorncrest, were simply seeking to unite two wealthy families to the aggrandizement of both?

Not for nothing was Almack's known as the Marriage Mart: its chief purpose was to sell the daughters of the nobility to the highest bidder. The glittering gaiety suddenly appeared artificial to Jodie, as she curtsied and gracefully accepted the Beau's invitation to dance.

Mrs. Carpenter's ball set the seal on Jodie's dissatisfaction. Dancing the nights away was all very well but London provided a hundred other amusements, and she was missing them.

With his rakish reputation, Lord Thorncrest undoubtedly was familiar with the places she wanted to visit.

"Will you take me to the Royal Saloon?" she asked the earl as they stood awaiting their turn to swing up the set.

"The Royal Saloon? Lord no. You cannot know what you are asking."

"I know perfectly well. I want to see it."

"Miss Judith, I have grown accustomed to your occasional lack of decorum, but be assured that to be seen in such a place would put you beyond the pale. Do not look to me to take you anywhere so disreputable," he paused, "at least while you share a roof with my betrothed."

Jodie did not care for the gleam in his eye as he added that qualification.

At the end of the dance, she found herself near Emily and abandoned the earl without a backward glance.

"Your fiancé is absolutely maddening," she fumed.

"*Fiancé?* Affianced? You mean Thorncrest?"

"Is 'fiancé' not anglicized yet? Yes, Thorncrest."

"What has he done?" Emily enquired. "I must say that I am quite out of temper with him, too. At supper I asked him about the Corn Laws and listened to his opinion. I have very strong views on the Corn Laws, but when I attempted to express them, he simply patted my hand and told me not to worry my pretty little head. I wanted to kick him under the table but in these thin slippers I should only have bruised my toes."

"Let's go home," Jodie proposed. "I want to speak to Giles before he retires for the night. I daresay Charlotte will be glad to leave."

They made their way to where Charlotte was sitting. Roland was beside her, having forsaken the card room to keep her company. In his presence they could not explain that they wanted to depart because they were annoyed with the earl.

"Charlotte dear, you look unwell," Emily improvised.

"Not unwell, merely a little tired," Jodie contradicted, seeing Roland's alarm. "It would be unconscionable of us to keep you from your rest. We shall not repine at leaving early, shall we, Emily?"

"Oh no, indeed I am a little fatigued myself."

With a disbelieving look, Charlotte collected her fan and her reticule. They took their leave of their hostess and drove home to Grosvenor Street.

As the carriage pulled up in front of the house, Jodie was glad to see a light in the window of the book room. It seemed a long time since she had had a proper talk with Giles, but if he acceded to her proposal she would be seeing a lot more of him.

= 10 =

GILES LOOKED UP as Jodie came into the room. In her ball gown, the sheen of silk glimmering gold in the lamplight, she was a vision of loveliness. All the same, he couldn't help remembering the glimpse of her scantily-clad body he had had in the Waterstock stables. It seemed like years ago.

He put down his pen and smiled at her as she rustled towards him.

"How is it going?" she asked, perching on a corner of the desk in thoroughly twentieth-century style.

"Plodding along. The material is fascinating, but it's very frustrating to have only the slide rule to work it out on." He wished he could tell her that the problems were solved, that he was taking her home. "From a more practical point of view, I'm sorry but we still don't know if we're going to find the answers."

She leaned towards him to lay a slender hand on his wrist, warm and comforting. "Don't worry about it, Giles. I didn't come here to bug you about it. One day at a time. You're working far too hard; you really must take some time off."

"Perhaps I will, if you promise to dance with me. How was the ball?"

She pulled a face, wrinkling her enchanting nose. "It's just like Disneyland, a lot of fun but once a year is plenty. There are so many other things I want to do and see."

"Such as?" he asked warily, warned by her off-hand tone that he might not like what was coming.

"Oh, Gentleman Jackson's and Tattersall's, for instance."

"Am I right in thinking that Charlotte would be scandalized?"

"Well yes, but I have seen most of the respectable amusements. Honestly, Giles, those places may be shocking to a gently bred nineteenth-century female, but I'm not one."

"Tell me about them."

"Then come and sit comfortably by the fire so that I don't get a crick in my neck watching your horrified reactions."

He was amused to see that Jodie made no attempt to curl up in the chair with her feet under her. He wondered whether she was simply being careful of an expensive silk frock or if she had unconsciously adapted to her environment, at least to that extent. Even taking her historical interests into account, she was coping admirably with the peculiarities of life in 1816.

He slouched back, his legs stretched before him. "Let's hear the worst."

"I'm afraid Tattersall's and Gentleman Jackson's are not the worst. One's a highly respectable horse auctioneer and the other an amateur boxing saloon."

"Would you walk into a men's gym in twentieth-century California?" Giles was genuinely curious. He wouldn't put it past her if she had what she considered a good reason.

"Well, no. Only in an emergency, I guess."

"Then suppose I go to the boxing place and report to you."

"Would you, Giles? You are a dear. But I cannot see why I should not go to Tattersall's. I think ladies do go to race meetings. Certainly Ada Lovelace does in the 1840s. I'll ask Charlotte about that."

"I can't help feeling I still haven't heard the worst."

"Most of the places are not that bad, just out of bounds for decorous young ladies. I *am* trying to be careful of my reputation, you know. But I'd love to see the inside of a gentleman's club, and the coffee houses and coaching inns in the City, and the Royal Saloon. And though I'd rather not, I feel I ought to visit the Cockpit."

"Cock fighting?" Giles was glad to hear the disgust in Jodie's voice. "You do take your research seriously. Tell me, are you planning to visit these places alone?"

"I asked Thorncrest to take me to the Royal Saloon, but he refused. I'll go alone if I have to."

He hid his amusement at her hopeful tone—so *that* was why she was concerned that he was working too hard. "Thorncrest is not known for his observance of propriety," he pointed out. "Just what goes on at this Royal Saloon?"

"The usual gambling and drinking," said Jodie airily.

"And? I'll ask Harry Font if you don't come clean."

"It's a haunt of the muslin company."

Giles had neither the time nor the background to delve into the mysteries of Regency slang. "Is the muslin company what I think it is?"

"Probably. It's one of many euphemisms for prostitutes. They have free entry to the Royal Saloon, though I don't know if the proprietor gets a rake-off or they are simply an added attraction."

"All right, I'll do my best to take you to those other places, or some of them at least, but I draw the line at a brothel."

"House of ill fame. The Royal Saloon isn't that. Half the peerage goes there to gamble. There are much worse places I've read about, I assure you, like the Finish and Old Mother Damnable's. I wouldn't dream of going there, even if it meant everlasting fame as a historian."

"Thank heaven for small mercies. I'll make enquiries about the Royal Saloon, but promise me that if I decide against it, you won't go alone."

She looked at him dubiously, her head cocked, her dark eyes serious. "It would leave a great hole in my research, not to have visited a gambling hall."

"Please, Jodie. From what I've heard, the streets of London now are not very different from the streets of Manhattan in our time. Your research will do you no good if you're lying dead in some back alley. Be reasonable."

"If Dian Fossey had felt that way . . ."

"Damn Dian Fossey!" He wanted to shake her. Important as her work was to her, its value was academic, not to be compared in his view with Fossey's discoveries about gorillas. Definitely not worth losing her life for as Fossey had—not that he would ever tell her so. Yet simply being here in 1816 was a risk, and it was his fault that she was here. Torn between guilt and annoyance, he stood up and walked to the window, parted the curtains to glance into the street, then returned to lean against the fireplace mantel.

Jodie watched him in silence. Did she guess how much the thought of her being hurt appalled him?

Postpone the decision, he thought. Maybe he'd be able to take her home before it had to be made. "Let me make enquiries. We may be fighting over nothing."

"No." She shook her head determinedly. "It's not fair of me to leave you worrying about it when you have so much else on your mind. I promise. I will not go anywhere alone."

"Bless you." In his relief and gratitude, Giles had to restrain himself from sweeping her into his arms and kissing her thoroughly. "And I promise I won't decide without consulting you and without very good reason. All right, where and when do we start? You'll have to get hold of some trousers first."

"Trousers?" Jodie sounded as shocked as Charlotte would have at the notion. "I cannot wear trousers."

Giles laughed. "You'd better watch it. You're really absorbing the values of this society."

"No, I'm not," she said crossly, "or I wouldn't want to go to the Royal Saloon. You just took me by surprise. I guess I will have to dress as a man. Okay, I'll find some pants and a coat and hat. I'll have to keep my hair hidden. Drat, that's going to make things difficult. Even the most old-fashioned gentlemen no longer wear their hair long. What a pity men don't still wear wigs."

"Footmen do. How would you like to be my footman?" he suggested teasingly.

"That's a splendid notion," she responded, to his astonishment. Excited, she rose from her chair in one swift, graceful movement, and moved to the fire, holding out one hand to the warmth and using the other to punctuate her points. "In the first place, I can get a livery made up, saying it's for a fancy-dress ball. And no one looks at a footman's face, so if we meet someone I've danced with they won't recognize me. Nor is anyone who matters likely to try to start a conversation with a footman so there won't be awkward questions about my voice or accent."

"Sounds good," he admitted.

"You're brilliant, Giles, even if by accident." She reached up and kissed his cheek. A sisterly kiss. He reciprocated with a brotherly hug.

At least, he hoped it was brotherly. When she stepped back quickly he was afraid he had put more enthusiasm into the brief embrace than he had intended. "If I'm going to be painting the town red with you in the near future, I'd better turn my brilliance back to my equations now," he said, moving towards the desk.

"It's much too late. You'll ruin your eyesight."

"But Mother, can't I just finish one eentsy little equation? Pleeease."

"Oh, very well. As long as you eat your carrots tomorrow like a good boy." Laughing, she departed.

Giles sat down at the desk and picked up his quill, then set it down again. Leaning back, he tilted the chair and put his feet on the desk, his hands locked behind his head. He gazed into the glowing embers in the grate.

He had addressed Jodie as "Mother," but her remark had first struck him as wifely. It was time he sorted out his feelings for her.

She alternately infuriated and delighted him. Her willingness to argue and her blithe dismissal of danger were maddening. On the other hand, he admired her independence, her dedication to her profession, her cheerfulness in the extraordinary circumstances in which they found themselves. She was kind; look at the way she had taken Emily and Charlotte under her wing. And she was beautiful.

His abdominal muscles tensed at the thought. He wanted her. He had never felt quite the same way towards another woman, this combination of affection and desire. . . .

He swung his feet violently to the floor, letting the chair fall with a thump. If and when they returned home it would be time enough to think on those lines. In the meantime, he must keep his imagination in check and remember that Jodie was his sister.

When he first saw her in livery, Giles found it easy to imagine Jodie as a naughty little sister. He had just walked back from Dover Street through torrential rain and was heading for his chamber to change for dinner. Emily peeked out of her dressing room, giggling, and beckoned to him.

"Come and see."

Intrigued, he followed her despite the discomfort of his damp clothes. "What is it?"

"Hush. Charlotte has gone to some dinner party with Roland, but Matty might tell her."

Draped in a sheet, Jodie was seated at the dressing table while Emily's abigail tied back her powdered hair with a black ribbon. Dinah carefully removed the sheet and Jodie stood up. She was wearing a calf-length bottle-green coat, liberally adorned with black braid, beneath which little was visible but a pair of shapely ankles in white stockings.

She bowed. As the skirts of the coat fell open, Giles saw that she had on black knee-breeches, cut full and unrevealing.

"Well, what do you think?" she demanded, mischief sparkling in her eyes.

"That colour doesn't suit you." He ducked, protecting his head, as all three females advanced on him with threatening gestures. "No, seriously, you make a passable youth, Jodie. Walk across the room. Women walk differently from men."

"My hat, Dinah." Jodie took a black tricorne from the abigail and placed it at a jaunty angle on her head, then pulled on white gloves. She strode across the small room, turned, and looked at him enquiringly.

"Not bad. That coat's long and loose enough to cover a multitude of sins." Giles stepped aside as the door beside him began to open.

"Dinah?" Matty peeped in. "Oh, beg pardon, Miss Emily, I just . . . Miss Judith? Lawks, what's to do?"

Giles took cowardly refuge behind the door. Dinah bustled forward and swept the older abigail with her into the hall, firmly closing the door behind them.

Approximately two seconds later, three ears were pressed to the door.

"Were that Miss Judith?" Matty asked plaintively. "Or is me eyes playing tricks on me?"

"'Tis only a fancy dress for a maskyrade, Matty."

"Dress! Fancy britches more like. And not a word has my lady said to me of any maskewrade."

"O' course not. Only Miss Judith and Mr. Giles is invited acos—acos it's that American lady as invited them," Dinah invented quick-wittedly. "You know, the widow Mr. Giles is courting."

"Mrs. Brown? What I heard is he's got a bit o' competition from Lord Font. I misdoubt she'll go for the title."

"More like she'll take her own countryman."

Embarrassing as he found the revelation that the servants were gossiping about his chances with Cassandra, Giles was glad that the subject of Jodie in livery had been dropped. He was about to relieve the pressure on his ear and the crick in his neck when Matty took up the thread again.

"That's as may be. Them Americans is odd folk. You know Miss Judith's not up to snuff, Dinah. Did you or Miss Emily tell her as it ain't proper for a lady to wear britches?"

"It's a maskyrade. No one won't know who she is."

"Decent's decent and indecent's indecent, maskewrade or no. My lady won't like it one bit."

"Now, Matty, there's no call to be a-worriting her lady-ship, in her condition. Miss Judith's not going to come to harm with her own brother to watch over her."

"And him with his head in the clouds and his eyes on the widow," Matty snorted. "Still an' all, you're right 'bout my lady. It won't do to have her put in a tizzy in her condition. But you warn Miss Judith what I said, mind!"

"I'll tell her, right enough. What was it you wanted me for?"

"My lady tore a bit o' Valenciennes. You're better at stitching up lace nor ever I'll be."

"I'll do it for you, Matty," Dinah promised. "Just set it aside. I better get back to Miss Emily."

The three eavesdroppers hurriedly moved away from the door as it opened, but Emily let the cat out of the bag.

"That was very clever of you, Dinah, to think of saying the invitation was from Mrs. Brown."

Giles felt his face grow red. "But I'm *not* courting her," he said with unnecessary vigour, glancing at Jodie to see how she took his denial.

"What does Matty mean, I'm not up to snuff!" she said indignantly, more concerned, to Giles's slight disappointment, with the affront to herself than with the suggestion that he fancied Cassandra. "I know perfectly well that wearing trousers is indecent."

Giles looked at her and started laughing; Emily joined in, and the maid hid a discreet snicker behind her hand. After a moment, Jodie grinned.

"All right, that was a pretty stupid thing to say. I guess Mom was right that eavesdroppers never hear any good of themselves."

" 'Head in the clouds,' " Giles quoted Matty, then sneezed. "Well, there are plenty of clouds out there for me to lose my head in."

"You are wet through," Jodie exclaimed. "I did not realize. You must go and change at once."

"Yes, I'd better. My umbrella blew inside out. It seems to rain every day—I can't remember such a dismal spring. I hope it clears up soon."

"It won't." Jodie was positive. "I had not thought about it, but 1816 became known as the year without a summer. Tambora erupted last year and threw so much junk into the atmosphere that it's keeping out the sun's heat. Frosts in July and . . ."

"I do not think I want to know," said Emily, putting her hands over her ears.

Giles agreed with her. If he and Jodie were to be stuck in the past, he had no desire to learn more of the future than the vague overall picture of English history that he remembered from school.

After dinner that evening, they discussed where to start their exploration of the seamier side of London. Jodie wanted to go to the Cockpit, "to get it over with," but Giles insisted that she must practise the rôle of footman somewhere innocuous first. Emily supported him. Though shocked by the whole enterprise, she did her best to help, accepting that standards would be different in the future.

Giles was proud of his great^n-aunt's understanding and discernment.

In the end, he and Jodie decided to go next evening to the City coffee-houses. Jodie begged off the rout to which the others were going, claiming that she needed to bring her journal up to date. With Dinah's assistance they slipped from the house unseen.

Giles waved his cane to summon a passing hackney and they were on their way.

Somewhat to his surprise Giles enjoyed their tour of the City coffee-houses, the Rainbow, Jonathan's, and Don Saltero's, where merchants and lawyers and clerks dined. He found the business discussions as dull as in his own time, but the political talk and the gossip about the latest news were interesting, particularly in comparison with the views of the Beau Monde. Jodie was fascinated. Her fingers twitched in her eagerness to write down her impressions.

No one spared her a second glance in her livery.

"It worked," she crowed as they headed homeward. "But I cannot see how anyone could bear to powder their hair. It itches abominably. Thank heaven the Faringdales have a shower bath."

Dinah let them into the house. Most of the servants were already abed, and the family had not yet returned. With care and luck, Giles decided, they might get away with a few more expeditions.

Anything was better than taking the risk that Jodie might go alone.

═ 11 ═

THE COCKPIT WAS on the south side of St. James's Park, where the pleasure grounds of the upper classes met the slums of Westminster. The crowd in attendance when Giles and Jodie entered the hall reflected this dichotomy.

Bucks of the Fancy in elegant coats made by Stultz or Milne rubbed shoulders with disreputable characters who looked as if they had found their rags in the gutters. Jodie's was by no means the only livery present. The hubbub of voices shouting out wagers, or vituperation, or encouragement to the contestants ranged from cant in the refined tones of Mayfair through the slow speech of countrymen to near incomprehensible Cockney. Occasionally, a whiff of sandalwood breached the fetid odour of unwashed bodies and tallow-dipped torches.

"Great," breathed Jodie in Giles's ear.

Fighting the urge to hold his nose, he wondered whether she spoke ironically or if the opportunity for research outweighed the atmosphere.

The aisle they stood in was as full of people as the benches on either side. Being taller than most, Giles could see that the tiered seats ringed an arena, where even now a dead bird was being removed and fresh sawdust scattered over a pool of blood. Feeling sick, he turned away.

"I don't know if I'll be able to find you a seat where you can see," he said, his head close to hers to be heard above the racket.

"I prefer not to see the ring. Brad took me to a bullfight in TJ once."

"TJ?" It was really Brad he wanted to know about, but he decided to stow the name away in his mind for future consideration.

"Tijuana. It's just across the Mexican border from San Diego. The *corrida* was quite the most disgusting thing I've ever seen and I'm sure a cockfight is as bad. It's the people I want to watch here."

"Unless you close your eyes, you can hardly help watching the people," he said. "Some of them are pretty disgusting too."

" 'Ere, mate, watch 'oo you're insulting," genially protested a ferret-faced man in a short coat and a hat with a drooping brim. "Want a tip fer the next main? You lay yer blunt on the blue an' you won't regret it, or my name ain't Jem Bloggs." With a wink, he slipped away through the crowd.

Giles disregarded this advice. He had little money in his pocket for despite Roland's generosity he refused to take a shilling more than he absolutely had to. In theory it might be his own inheritance, but in practice it belonged to the present viscount and was not Giles's to gamble with.

Grasping Jodie's braided sleeve, he battled his way along the nearest row of benches tugging her behind him. A broad-beamed fellow who looked like a prosperous farmer stood up as they approached him and hallooed to someone in the opposite direction. Giles dodged into his seat as he stumped away with the irresistible impetus of a rolling boulder, eliciting catcalls as he trampled feet in his path.

There was room for Jodie to squeeze in beside him. She took off her hat and fanned herself.

"I am dying of heat in this coat."

"Don't you dare unbutton it."

She sighed. "I suppose I had best not, though I cannot believe anyone would notice."

Giles stood up and looked around, carefully averting his eyes from the mayhem going on below.

"There's more space up higher, but it will be hotter," he shouted down at her. "Oh hell!" He sat down abruptly. "Lord Alfred, and he's seen me. He's coming this way. Keep your head down, Jodie."

96

"Lord Alfred? That guy I danced with the other night who trod all over my new slippers?"

"Yes, the one who interrogated me about the War of 1810."

"1812." Jodie giggled. "I've never in my life heard so many platitudes about international friendship spouted in a quarter-hour. What is he doing here? He struck me as a nice, naïve boy who would not hurt a fly, unless it happened to get under the sole of his shoe." She jammed her hat on her head, tilting it forwards to shade her face.

Unfortunately Giles's neighbour departed at that moment and Lord Alfred took his place.

"Good to see someone I know," he said, somewhat breathless after his struggle through the crowd. "What d'you think of the sport?"

Momentarily Giles debated his answer. Honesty won. "I consider it an abomination and I'm about to leave. I must confess to some curiosity which is more than quenched, so I hope you'll excuse me, my lord."

"It's those iron spurs they put on the cocks nowadays have spoiled it," said the young man agreeably. "Give me a good terrier and I'd rather go ratting. Mind if I go with you?"

"Not at all," said Giles, unable to think of a reason to object.

Jodie appeared to be examining her knees with the greatest interest. He stuck his elbow in her ribs and hissed, "Follow us," then pushed past her, heading for the exit. At frequent intervals he turned his head, purportedly to speak to Lord Alfred, actually to see if Jodie was managing to make her way after them. The black tricorne bobbed along in their wake.

It was raining when the trio emerged from the building. What rotten luck to land in the year without a summer, Giles thought gloomily, looking around for a taxi. A hackney.

"What say to supper at the Piazza?" suggested Lord Alfred with unabated good cheer.

Jodie tugged on Giles's coattail, an unmistakable but uninterpretable signal. Probably she wanted to go to the Piazza coffee house, which she had mentioned as a haunt of Byron and his friends. She must be mad. In a well-lit room Lord Alfred was bound to recognize her.

"Thank you, my lord, but I'd best be getting home, if I can only find a hackney."

"Won't hear of it, my dear fellow. My man will have my rig round in a trice and I'll run you home. International friendship and all that nonsense."

"That's good of you, only I have my footman with me." Noting his lordship's surprise, he added, "I'm not too familiar with the town as yet."

"So that's what the fellow's up to skulking behind us. He can hop on behind with my groom. Here they are."

A light town carriage drove up, splashing dirty water from a string of puddles so filthy they failed to gleam in the wavering light of the oil-burning street lamps. Giles eyed the high perch at the back with some misgiving. Jodie would be soaked to the skin, yet he could not ask for her to ride inside, nor even help her up without arousing suspicion.

He grinned as she cast him a fulminating glance and scrambled up to join the groom. This whole caper was her notion; she would have to abide by the consequences.

To his relief, Lord Alfred did not interrogate him about America again. It was almost as difficult to avoid accepting any of the many invitations the young man proffered. He managed to escape without committing himself to anything specific while leaving the impression that he would be delighted to join in a spree with his lordship and his cronies.

"My compliments to Miss Judith," said Lord Alfred as the carriage pulled up in Grosvenor Street. "I'm not much in the petticoat line but I like a filly with a bit of spirit."

"I'll convey your compliments to my sister," Giles assured him, stepping out into the downpour.

He dashed for the shelter of the front door overhang. Dinah would be waiting down at the basement door in the area, but it would never do to let Lord Alfred see him go down there.

Glancing back to make sure Jodie was following, he saw her start down the area steps. A moment later a very twentieth-century curse floated up to him. The carriage was moving away, so he hurried down, to find Jodie seated on the flagstones.

"That was the only bit of me not totally sodden," she said crossly.

He was shaking with silent laughter as he helped her up. She hobbled ahead of him towards the door that Dinah was opening.

"Oh, miss, you'll catch your death," exclaimed the maid, predictably.

"To think I thought that wretched man was cute," Jodie growled.

"He asked me to convey his compliments," Giles told her. "He likes a spirited filly."

"A *what*?" she demanded in disgust, helping Dinah unbutton her coat. "Did he really say that? I shall never speak to him again. Do you realize he left his unfortunate groom huddled in the street waiting to run for his carriage the minute he stepped out of the cockpit? And that the reason he dislikes the use of metal spurs in cockfights is that they kill the birds quicker? I was never so disillusioned in my life."

"What, never? What about when Brad took you to the bullfight?"

"He thought it was gross too. If he hadn't, I'd have dumped him like a ton of hot bricks. Probably. He was a cool guy, mostly."

"Was?"

"Was. We had a disagreement about my coming to England," Jodie answered tersely.

It was impossible to be jealous of a past relationship, Giles assured himself as they sneaked up the back stairs. Nonetheless, knowing the name of her boyfriend disturbed him in a way that knowing she had slept with some unnamed male had not. He did not subscribe to the double standard prevalent in this age, yet he wished Brad had remained anonymous.

Jodie was absolutely determined to see the Royal Saloon, but Giles had been avoiding the subject for days. One morning she pounced on him as he was about to leave the house to go to Dover Street to consult Cassandra, as he still did most days.

"I am going with you. It is time I paid my respects to Mrs. Brown. I am already dressed for walking and Dinah is ready to go too, so there can be no possible objection."

Giles smiled his crooked smile. "Have I voiced any objection? I shall be glad of the company. You won't need Dinah, though. I'm only going to drop off some calculations for Cassandra to check against her own, then I'll walk back with you."

For once it was not raining, though the sky was grey and an icy wind whistled round the corners. Jodie hugged her warm cloak about her.

"Charlotte and Roland are going to some grand affair tomorrow to which we are not invited," she opened as they turned down Davies Street. "It is the perfect opportunity to go to the Royal Saloon."

"I've been asking around and I gather it's not the most respectable of places even for gentlemen."

"I told you, it is frequented by half the peerage."

"That just means it's more likely that someone will recognize you. We can't count on getting away as easily as we did with Lord Alfred at the Cockpit."

"Easily! Speak for yourself. I was snuffling for three days and the bruises on my rear end lasted a week."

"That proves my point. You don't want to go through that again."

"No one cast a second glance my way at Tattersall's, which was swarming with gentlemen, nor at the coaching inns."

"Which were swarming with pickpockets," Giles snorted.

Jodie grinned. A footman's pockets had not been deemed worthy of picking. "You only lost a half crown," she soothed him. "And when the next one tried, you caught him a crack with your cane he will not forget in a hurry, I vow."

"There are worse hazards than pickpockets at the Royal Saloon. Harry Font told me it's notorious for card-sharping, drunkenness and debauchery."

"Unless you mean to play or drink or chase the Cyprians, there is nothing to worry about."

"But you . . ."

"I have no intention of doing any of those things, I promise, especially not the last," Jodie teased. His concern for her was endearing but irritating. "Nor will seeing them hurt me, if that is what upsets you. I doubt there is anything worse than what I have seen on TV or in the movies. You are absorbing the values of the day as you said I was. Remember—I have no refined sensibilities."

"None at all."

His remark hurt her. Still, if he thought her hard and unfeeling, changing her mind would not change his. She pressed on. "Please, Giles. I promised not to go alone, and I shall not, but I have had to give up hope of White's and Watier's and the other clubs, since you can only go in as guest of a member. The Royal Saloon is the least disreputable of the gambling hells open to the public."

"It's useless trying to protect you, isn't it?" He sighed. "All my gentlemanly instincts going to waste."

Reassured, she said severely, "You are quizzing me. You will take me, then?"

"If you can get away tonight."

"I am not sure. Why?"

"Harry Font is coming up from Kent tomorrow and we'll be comparing results into the early hours."

"Coming up from Kent! I thought he was in London."

"He comes and goes. It's only a few miles to Font Hall."

"So you have been seeing Cassandra alone."

"Good lord, no. If Harry's not there, we are closely chaperoned by his Aunt Tavie, I assure you. I've never been alone with Cassandra for a moment."

Jodie tried to hide her relief. "Aunt Tavie—she is the rheumaticky old lady?"

"Yes, and a veritable dragon, though she's Harry's favourite relative, I gather. They have been waiting for the weather to improve before taking her down to Font Hall to attend their wedding. I haven't mentioned your 'year without a summer.'"

"Nor shall I. I daresay there must be moments when it is not quite so horrid. How are your calculations going? I don't ask more often because I don't want to hassle you, not because I am not interested."

"I would report more often, if there were anything to report. We are progressing, but slowly. At our present rate, it'll be ten days or so before we can be sure whether it's possible or not."

"Whether it's possible to go home? Of course, you would have told me if you'd figured that out for sure. I guess that's another reason I haven't asked—I didn't want to know." Hearing a tremor in her own voice, Jodie added as brightly as she could manage, "Luckily I'm beginning to feel quite at home here."

Giles seemed to guess that she needed comfort, since he could not offer reassurance. He put one arm round her shoulders and gave her a quick hug.

When they reached the house in Dover Street, Cassandra invited them to go in for refreshments. In her reserved way she seemed pleased to see Jodie, who at once felt guilty for not having called sooner. Though Cassandra had chosen her exile, Jodie realized she would naturally be glad to talk to a woman from her own time, and about subjects other than physics.

It turned out that their chief topic was plumbing. Cassandra was vastly envious of the Faringdales' water closets and shower bath, and when she described the misery of washing her hair in a copper tub, Jodie was not surprised.

They also talked of clothes. Cassandra seemed to be as unaware of the "future history" of fashion as she was of the general course of events in nineteenth-century England. Remembering Emily's distaste for hints of the future, Jodie did not enlighten her. She did not need to know that in a couple of years heavy whalebone corsets would once more be *de rigueur* and that women's clothes would grow ever more elaborate and confining, culminating in the virtual imprisonment of the bustle and crinoline.

"I do miss the comfort of pants," Cassandra admitted, "but Harry has agreed that once we are married I shall learn to ride astride in breeches as long as I stay on the estate. Do you ride?"

"No, but I shall certainly learn if we have to stay. In fact, even if we go back I hope to learn. Giles has horses at Waterstock."

They both glanced at Giles. He was keeping the old ladies nobly entertained, to judge by Aunt Seppie's titter and Aunt Tavie's cackle. Cassandra turned back to Jodie with an understanding look.

"I wish you luck, my dear," she said in a low voice.

Jodie decided she liked Cassandra immensely. If she and Giles could not go home it would be a relief to have a friend to whom she could talk unreservedly.

As they were taking their leave, Giles asked what time Harry was expected on the morrow.

"I'm glad you asked, I nearly forgot to tell you," Cassandra exclaimed. "I received a note from him this morning. He's been detained and he cannot be here until the day after tomorrow. I hope that will not inconvenience you?"

"Not at all," Giles assured her. "We can only be grateful that the two of you are so generous with your time and expertise. Right, Jodie?"

She agreed fervently.

As soon as the front door closed behind them, Jodie gave a little skip of excitement.

"So I need not try to fabricate an excuse for this evening. We can go to the Royal Saloon tomorrow night when Roland and Charlotte are out."

"The Royal Saloon tomorrow," Giles agreed unwillingly.

═ 12 ═

THE ROYAL SALOON was situated in Piccadilly, a street that started out nobly at the Hyde Park turnpike but lost most of its pretensions to grandeur by the time it ended at Haymarket.

This was not to say that the Royal Saloon had no pretensions to grandeur. A fashionable haunt of the nobility despite its ill repute, it was decorated in vaguely eastern style, featuring pagodas and bamboo and lotus blossoms with a few sinuous dragons twining about for good measure. Jodie rather liked the palm trees—they reminded her of California.

The busiest hours, she had heard, were between midnight and dawn. Though it was still early when she and Giles arrived, as they had to be home well before that hour, the main room was already well-populated. Women in gaudy, spangled gowns with alarming décolletés sauntered arm in arm between the scattered tables. At some of these gentlemen sat ogling the parading beauties. The occupants of others were more interested in conversation, or their lobster dinners, or the contents of the bottles delivered by scurrying waiters.

As she followed Giles down the room, Jodie noticed that a few of the Cyprians had already found their marks and were seated at tables, some on chairs and some, simpering, on pantaloon-clad knees. Here and there a low-cut bodice had fulfilled its function by spilling its contents. Jodie quickly averted her eyes.

Giles found a small table in an ill-lit corner and sat down.

He beckoned to Jodie and she leaned towards him at a properly respectful angle, as if to receive his orders.

"I should think you'd better stand against the wall behind me," he whispered, "Like those other footmen over there." He nodded towards the far side of the room.

Jodie saw a couple of men in livery and powdered hair, waiting like statues until their masters should need them. "Not *other* footmen, *real* footmen," she whispered back. "I'll never manage to stand that still."

"Just don't scratch," he advised.

A waiter was approaching so Jodie stepped back to the drapery-covered wall. She discovered that it was not a wall after all, just curtains covering an alcove from which issued squeals and giggles. Hastily she moved to her right until she reached a solid pier between the arches of two of the private chambers. Now that she knew what she was looking for, she realized that the main room was lined down both sides with curtained recesses and there were more on the balcony.

Judging by some of the activities proceeding in full view at the tables, the carryings-on in the alcoves were best concealed.

Jodie had a good view of the nearer part of the room, and the overall noise level was low enough to allow her to hear snatches of conversation. She was sufficiently familiar with the cant of the period to know that horse-racing and boxing were the chief topics, though the details escaped her.

The hum of voices was punctuated at frequent intervals by shouts of "Waiter!" All the waiters seemed—and needed—to be nimble little men with a magnificent sense of balance. They also all wore worried expressions, except that the one who had taken Giles's order now reappeared scowling. Jodie saw that Giles had asked for a tankard of ale. Being cheap it was doubtless unpopular with both proprietor and servants, promising little profit.

Most of the shouts were for champagne, brandy, or claret. The waiters were kept as busy removing empty bottles as providing full ones, and more than one gentleman's red face and glazed eyes suggested their owner would soon be under the table.

Jodie decided it was time to investigate the two doors leading off the back of the room. None of the unaccompanied lightskirts had ventured through either door, and most of the men going that way did not take their ladybirds with them. That must be where the serious gaming went on.

Jodie moved to Giles's side and adopted the deferential pose. "You called, sir?"

"As a matter of fact, no," he teased. "Go away."

"I want to see what is going on in the back rooms."

"I dread to think. Must you?"

"It's probably more decorous than in here."

"It could hardly be less. I rather fancy that redheaded wench over there."

Jodie followed his gaze, just in time to catch the cheerful wink aimed at Giles by a voluptuous lady of the night. As she swayed towards them her lime-green gown clung to every curve, and in contrast her hair blazed in the candlelight.

"Dyed," Jodie scoffed. "Come on."

With an exaggerated sigh, Giles rose and led the way, shaking his head with a mournful expression as they passed the redhead.

"Good luck, lovie," she wished him. "Come back when you've lined your pockets. Just ask for Fifi." She smiled at the footman following him, then her kohl-ringed eyes widened and she looked Jodie up and down. Grinning, she put a finger to her lips. "Already taken, is 'e, ducks?" she whispered. "Don't worry, I'm no poacher. It's the legs gives it away but none of them won't notice." Her sweeping gesture expressed supreme contempt for every male in the place.

"Ta, love," Jodie whispered back, and hurried after Giles.

The room they entered was hushed, an occasional exclamation of pleasure or dismay rising above the rattle and click of dice, the shuffling of cards, the gurgle of bottle and glass. There was an odd squeaky sound Jodie could not identify, until she saw that some of the gamblers were keeping score on slates.

It was too quiet to risk telling Giles that Fifi had seen through her disguise. He was looking around the room as if searching for someone but it would soon become noticeable if he did not sit down to play. Jodie concentrated on mentally cataloguing the furnishings and the players as fast as possible, then tugged unobtrusively on his sleeve. She could feel his tension.

He turned and went out into the main room. The din had grown louder, unless it was just in contrast to the card room's quiet. No, a couple of bucks were shouting at each other across a table.

Jodie was glad of Giles's tall figure just in front of her. She nearly stopped him to tell him about Fifi but he would undoubtedly insist on leaving at once. Though she was far from reluctant, she must just take a peek at the other room first. She followed as close to his heels as she dared.

The room was dedicated to billiards. A reasonably competent pool player, Jodie watched with interest. At the nearest table a game was just beginning. The white ball swished across the smooth green baize and hit the red with a clunk. Both balls rebounded and rolled down the table, coming to rest behind a line drawn from side to side. A murmur of appreciation and scattered applause from the spectators told Jodie it was a good shot.

The player straightened with an air of nonchalant smugness. It was Lord Thorncrest.

His gaze slid across Jodie's face—and returned. His expression changed to astonished incredulity. She had no doubt whatsoever that he had recognized her.

He looked at Giles and his eyebrows rose in the familiar cynical arrogance. For a moment the two men stared at each other, then Giles turned and walked calmly to the door. Jodie had to force herself not to beat him to it.

As they entered the main room, one of the two bucks she had noticed before, now standing, aimed a blow at the other across their table. The second responded in kind. A chair went over and hit a waiter behind the knees, sending him to the floor. His tray went flying. It slid across another table, scattering bottles, and hit the midriff of a large man with a broken nose. As he surged to his feet, a ferocious scowl on his misshapen face, his table toppled and females fled screaming.

Giles grabbed Jodie's hand and started round the melée. Fists were swinging in all directions. Several of the *filles de joie* joined in, pulling hair and scratching, and screeching imprecations. An incensed waiter brought down his laden tray on the head of a nearby gentleman. Glass crunched underfoot and fumes of spilt liquor made Jodie dizzy.

She hung on tight. Giles glanced round at her and failed to see a harpy standing on a table in his path, aiming a broken chair at all and sundry with joyous abandon. The deafening hubbub drowned Jodie's shout of warning.

The chair was inches from Giles's head when Fifi's colourful curls appeared from beneath the table; she seized the ankle of the woman wielding the chair and pulled. They both went over with the chair on top of them.

Jodie was prepared to swear that as she raced past she saw Fifi wink at her.

Everyone was far too busy to notice a gentleman running hand-in-hand with his footman. They kept running until they reached the street and leaned against a wall, panting.

"That is positively and absolutely the last place I take you sightseeing," said Giles.

Jodie giggled. "It started as a sort of '60s love-in and ended as a barroom brawl straight out of a Western movie. Do you realize you would have been conked on the head if it wasn't for Fifi?"

"Fifi? The gorgeous redhead? No, I didn't see that. Bloody hell, I've left my overcoat and cane in there. I'll have to get them. You wait here and don't you dare move a single step, unless you see an empty hackney."

While he was gone, a carriage drove up and disgorged a party of young men already half-seas over. Jodie wished she could fade into the wall, but they did not spare her a glance as they staggered past her, singing raucously in several different keys. Giles returned a moment later with coat and cane.

"No hackneys? I've no desire to hang about here, let's start walking. Thank heaven it's not raining for once. Tell me about Fifi."

"She guessed I'm not a man."

"Bloody hell, are you serious?"

"She didn't give me away. She was kind of nice."

"You were lucky," he said grimly. "I don't imagine Thorncrest will give you away either, since you're his fiancé's cousin, but sooner or later you're bound to meet someone equally perceptive who isn't 'kind of nice.' That was positively . . ."

". . . And absolutely the last place you take me sightseeing," Jodie finished his sentence for him. She tucked her hand under his arm. "Do you think you could possibly walk a little slower so I can keep up and breathe at the same time? That's better. I don't blame you, Giles. You've been a real angel and don't think I don't appreciate it. I know it's gone against the grain to waste your time on such frivolous amusements."

He grinned down at her. "Actually, I've rather enjoyed myself. On the whole," he amended, "my life hasn't been entirely given up to serious pursuits, you know. Besides, our little adventures have had a serious purpose for you."

"I've enjoyed myself too," she admitted, "though it did get a bit hairy back there." It was funny in retrospect, but at the time she had been frightened—and very glad of Giles's presence. She was about to tell him so when he suddenly stood still.

"Sshhh."

The stealthy footsteps following them went on for a couple of paces, then sped up into a run.

"Muggers!" Giles swung round, his cane miraculously turning into a sword. "Three of them. Get behind me."

Even as he spoke another two men darted out of an alley ahead of Jodie and rushed towards her. The one on her right bore a cudgel. Cursing her heavy coat, Jodie took a deep breath, nerving herself to meet them.

Her back to Giles she corrected him in a voice that sounded startlingly calm to her ears: "Footpads."

Her ready stance gave the men pause. Their onrush slowed, then the unarmed man hissed, "Starkey said 'tis a gentry mort out for a lark."

Encouraged by the reminder that he faced a female, the other attacked. As the cudgel swung down towards her head, Jodie blocked his arm with crossed wrists and used its momentum to guide it down between his legs. He squawked in pain as he hit his own crotch with his forearm. The cudgel was behind him now. Jodie seized it in her left hand and conked her squirming victim on the back of the head. Continuing the smooth sequence of moves, she wheeled on the other man, who had incautiously decided to join the fray while she was otherwise engaged—he thought. She kicked him in the kneecap, saw him drop to the pavement with a squeal of agony, and still turned, glancing quickly back to make sure he was disabled.

Giles was facing two burly men, the thin steel of his rapier gleaming as it darted in a web of protection in front of him. Jodie's battle had taken only a few seconds, just long enough for the man nearest her to draw a knife. Preparing to throw it, he moved sideways towards Jodie as the other villain went in the opposite direction, dividing Giles's attention. The footpad with the knife was watching Giles. His head met Jodie's cudgel and he sank to the ground without a murmur.

Completing her turn, Jodie saw Giles's sword leap twice to slice his opponent's arm and leave a slashmark on his cheek. The man stumbled backwards, cursing. The lookout, a mere boy, had already taken to his heels. Jodie's first attacker was out cold, the second hobbling away with one leg dragging.

He turned and spat. "She-devil!"

"She-devil indeed," said Giles respectfully, wiping his sword blade on his handkerchief.

"No, I'm not." Jodie was shaking. "I was scared to death. Hold me a minute, Giles."

His weapon at the ready in his right hand, he gathered her to him with his left arm, murmuring words of comfort and admiration. She clung to him, aware that over her head he was watching the downed villains for signs of danger.

There was one danger he was not considering. If the Watch appeared, too late to help, and found him embracing his footman—well, this was not tolerant twentieth-century England. Rumours of Byron's homosexual activities had damned

110

him as surely as had the tales of incest, and proof could have hanged him, peer or no. Jodie pulled away from Giles.

"Thanks, I'm okay now. Let's get away from these creeps. I don't want to get mixed up with what passes for the police in this day and age." She picked up the lower part of his cane from the cobbles where he had tossed it. "Here. It's a good job there's no laws about concealed weapons."

Returning her strained smile, he put the swordstick back together then held out his arm. She shook her head and walked beside him, careful not to touch him, breathing deeply to try to still her racing pulse.

"Do you think your friend Fifi alerted them?" he proposed, his voice as unnaturally calm as her own. "I imagine they must have considered us easy prey."

"Yes, they probably only attack lone gentlemen. They would have thought a female no obstacle. I can't believe Fifi told them about me." She frowned. "No, Fifi thought me a lightskirt but the footpad called me a 'gentry mort,' which is slang for a lady. I expect they saw me holding your arm and heard me talking."

"Better keep your voice down then. Ah, there's a cab at last." He hailed the hackney, and when they were settled inside he went on, "Where did you learn the karate?"

"It's not real karate, I just took a self-defense course. What about you and the swordplay? It gave me quite a shock when your elegant cane turned into a lethal weapon."

"Harry said I should have something, and a pistol is hard to conceal. I learned to fence when I was a student in Germany. It's a popular sport there."

"You were magnificent."

"So were you. The Magnificent Two."

"Somehow it doesn't have the ring of the Magnificent Seven." Jodie pondered. "How about the Powerful Pair?"

"Not quite. The Courageous Couple?"

The word game dissipated Jodie's tension and she was laughing by the time she rejected 'the Redoubtable Duo' on the grounds that Batman and Robin were known as the Dynamic Duo. The hackney drew up before the Faringdales' house.

Her laughter faded suddenly.

"I've just thought," she said, trudging wearily down the steps to the area door. "Thorncrest may not want to blacken his fiancé's cousin's reputation in public, but there is nothing whatsoever to stop him telling Roland he saw me at the Royal Saloon."

"Don't worry about it. I'll take care of you," Giles said softly as the door opened to reveal Dinah's anxious face.

Even to an independent modern woman, his reassurance was sweet.

=== 13 ===

"I'M RIGHT GLAD you're home safe, miss," Dinah whispered to Jodie, "and Mr. Giles too. I've heard stories 'bout that place 'ud make your hair stand on end. Wicked, it is. Miss Emily's already gone up, but she said to be sure and ask you to go tell her everything."

On the way up the back stairs, Jodie swiftly expurgated their adventures of the evening. She would have liked to eliminate all mention of Lord Thorncrest's presence in that den of iniquity, but Emily ought to be forewarned. She was bound to come in for some awkward questions if her betrothed denounced Jodie to her brother.

Emily was sitting up in bed, swathed in a quilt. Jodie saw a book disappear into the folds as she entered.

"Oh, I was afraid it was Charlotte." The volume reappeared. "I did not want to upset her."

"What are you reading?" The scene was so normal, so cosy, Jodie found it hard to believe that a few minutes ago she had been fighting for her life.

"Mrs. Godwin's *Vindication of the Rights of Women*," said Emily guiltily. "She says . . ."

"Not now, I'm exhausted." Jodie let Dinah help her out of her coat and sank into a chair, rubbing her sore wrists. "We'll discuss it later, I promise you."

"What is wrong with your arms? Are you hurt? Let me see," Emily ordered, jumping out of bed. "You are horridly bruised. Dinah, fetch some arnica and witch hazel. Now, Jodie, tell me what happened."

Jodie obliged. While she spoke, Dinah returned, rubbed

arnica on her wrists, and bound them with bandages soaked in cool, medicinal-smelling witch hazel. She and Emily were a splendid audience, open-mouthed, their eyes growing rounder and rounder.

When all the horrified exclamations were over, Emily asked wistfully, "Did Lord Thorncrest have one of those women with him?"

"No, he was with several gentlemen, no females." She was glad to be able to answer honestly, and surprised at the question. Was it possible that Emily was developing a tendre for the earl?

She no longer feared him. Though she silently disagreed with his views on some subjects, she had learned that at least he studied and thought about serious matters. He drove her in the park and danced with her regularly, and was unfailingly courteous—indeed, she had not suffered the sharp edge of his tongue since the betrothal had been arranged.

Or since he had had Jodie to whet it on, thought that young lady with a secret grin. Maybe her plan was working. Maybe Emily was beginning to feel just a tad jealous of the attentions her betrothed paid to her supposed cousin.

After all, the wretched man was still handsome enough to dazzle the most sought-after young lady.

On the other hand, he had yet to listen to Emily's opinion on any subject, let alone ask for it. Nor did Jodie suppose, simply because he had not had a ladybird with him at the Royal Saloon, that the earl had mended his libertine ways in honour of his betrothal.

At that point in her cogitations, Jodie realized that her chin was resting on her chest. She jerked upright and opened her eyes.

"You *are* exhausted," Emily commiserated, "and no wonder. Off to bed with you."

Jodie hauled herself out of the chair. "How am I going to explain this to Charlotte?" she asked muzzily, holding out her linen-wrapped arms.

"You could tell her that you tripped over the hem of your gown going upstairs, and put out your arms to save yourself. She would accept it. Remember how you fell into Giles's arms that first morning?"

"Wretch! I learned weeks since how to manage long skirts properly."

"I doubt Charlotte will ask. She is aware that something has been going on and she prefers not to know the details. Dinah, I think you had best help Miss Judith to bed, if you please, or she is like to fall asleep on the floor."

When she awoke the next morning, Jodie could not remember undressing, let alone climbing into bed. She guessed from the sounds in the street that it was late. Though her wrists were merely stiff, not painful, she was drowsy and disinclined to move.

Dinah looked in, saw that she was awake, and came in.

"How you feeling, Miss Judith? Miss Emily left this for you." She searched the pocket of her apron and produced a twist of paper. "She's gone shopping with my lady, and Mr. Giles went off to Mrs. Brown's, and my lord's at his club. I'll bring your breakfast, shall I?" She pulled back the curtains, revealing another grey, drizzling day.

Jodie was ravenous, but the smell of liquor seemed to cling to her hair. "I shall take a shower bath first, then eat below stairs."

"I'll warm a towel for you, miss, while you read your note. 'Tis a miserable day, right enough."

Jodie smoothed the paper while the abigail bustled about. Emily wrote that she meant to beg off a visit to Charlotte's sister after shopping and she would come home to see that Jodie was all right. She had suggested to her sister-in-law that Jodie had probably stayed up late writing and would not want to be wakened to shop.

"Bless her," Jodie thought. She had no desire whatever to go shopping—every trifle she acquired seemed to anchor her in this time. Though she had accepted a ball gown and a few odds and ends from Charlotte, she still mostly wore dresses borrowed from Emily.

She took her shower, luxurious but brief. In the town-house, hot water was always available though limited in quantity. Emily's excuse for her sleeping late reminded her that she must write up a description of last night, so she had a breakfast tray brought to her in the book room and ate as she wrote.

Absorbed in her work, she vaguely heard voices in the entrance hall but took no notice until the book room door opened.

"Lord Thorncrest, miss," Potter announced. "Are you at home?"

He stepped back quickly as the earl walked past him and into the room.

"I feel sure Miss Judith will receive me," he drawled.

Jodie nodded reluctant assent and the butler left. She stuck her pen in the inkwell, stood up, and moved around the desk, nervous but refusing to be intimidated. What did he want with her? Despite his faults, he was too much the gentleman to stoop to blackmail.

"Good morning, my lord."

"Come now, Judith, such formality! My name is Charles, you may remember."

"I did not give you permission to use my name, sir."

"With women of your kind, my dear, one does not wait for permission," he said drily. With one stride he was at her side, and sweeping her into his arms he planted a passionate kiss on her lips.

For one startled moment Jodie responded. He was certainly an expert and she had no profound objection to being kissed. Then she recalled her situation—he was a notorious rake and she was a respectable young woman living under her cousin's protection.

To one who had routed three armed assailants a mere twelve hours since, a single would-be seducer was no problem. Lord Thorncrest landed on his back on the Axminster, astonishment and fury vying for command of his features.

"Want to try it again, brother?" Jodie asked dangerously.

"Bravo!" Giles had entered unnoticed. "Pray don't let me interrupt."

The earl bounded to his feet. "Faringdale—of course," he snarled. "I'll have your blood for this."

116

"By all means." Giles was ready to oblige. "But surely it is up to me to do the challenging. After all, you appeared to be manhandling my sister."

"You hit me and I demand satisfaction." Thorncrest felt his undamaged chin with a puzzled air. "Name your seconds."

"I didn't hit you. I expect my cousin and Lord Font will act for me."

"Oh no you don't," Jodie intervened. "This is my quarrel, Giles, and I can handle it."

"I've no doubt of that."

"Then there's no earthly reason you need to get mixed up in it."

"My honour as a gentleman," Giles pointed out, grinning.

"For heaven's sake, be serious. I know you can fence and shoot but Thorncrest has probably fought a dozen duels and you've never fought in earnest in your life. I bet you don't even know the proper etiquette."

"I am perfectly willing to follow American etiquette," said Lord Thorncrest stiffly. "I believe two of your politicians— Burns and Hamilton, was it?—met honourably some years since."

"Hamilton was killed and *Burr* discredited," Jodie pointed out. "Think, Giles. What the hell am I supposed to do if you end up dead or in Newgate?"

"I hardly think it'll come to that, but if so, Cassandra and Harry will see you get home safely."

"And then I suppose I go in to tea with your mother and tell her: 'I'm frightfully sorry, Lady Faringdale, but your son got himself pinked in a duel a couple of centuries ago and I had to leave him behind'?"

To her indignation, Giles laughed. "I have to admit even my imperturbable mother might be a bit put out. Don't worry, I left the keys in the car; you can skip tea and drive yourself back to Oxford."

"And have the cops after me for car theft and kidnapping?" Jodie was beginning to see the funny side. "Can't you just imagine the headlines? 'Physicist peer vanishes! U.S. coed questioned by Scotland Yard.' The gutter press would just love it."

"Coed's an American word. 'Lovely graduate,' they'd say, 'claims researcher jailed in 1816.' They like lovely, it's shorter than beautiful."

"'Historian runs amok, slays sexy scientist, hides body in past.' I can just see it on the front page of the tabloids at the supermarket checkout."

They had both forgotten the earl. Lord Thorncrest had lost his glower and was looking distinctly uneasy. Jodie's final remark was too much for him.

"I'm damned if I know what you're talking about, but I trust you mean to explain," he said, starting out belligerent but ending on a plaintive note.

Jodie and Giles stared at him in dismay.

"Oh lord!" Giles flopped into the nearest chair. "What did we say?" he asked Jodie.

She ran back over their nonsense in her mind. "Too much. We're going to have to give him some sort of explanation. For heaven's sake sit down, Thorncrest, don't stand there scowling at us."

He opened his mouth to protest, then meekly sat. She joined him on the leather sofa.

"This is all your fault," she accused him. "You shouldn't have assaulted me. I'm no feeble little debutante, you know."

"That much I had gathered, but what the devil *are* you?"

Jodie looked at Giles. He obliged.

"Jodie's a student of history at Oxford University. A graduate student—she already has her degree—and a superior student, since she won an important scholarship."

"Women up at Oxford? Gammon," said Lord Thorncrest bluntly.

"Perhaps I should have said 'Jodie *will be* a student.' We both come from the far end of the twentieth century." Giles paused, but the earl was too stunned to speak. "I am, or will be, Viscount Faringdale, a descendant of our present host. We were thrown back in time by an accident I can't even begin to explain to someone who has never spared the time for 'playing with numbers', as you once put it."

"Giles is not merely a useless aristocrat," Jodie put in,

making Thorncrest flush with annoyance. "He's a distinguished natural philosopher with a team of researchers working under him."

"And Jodie is not only a historian," Giles added, "but a student of the Japanese martial arts. Hence your recent tumble."

"I don't believe it. I don't believe a word of it."

Jodie jumped up and assumed a ready pose. "Want to try it again?"

"No, thank you." He slid away from her to the other end of the sofa. Unexpectedly he grinned. "I'll meet your brother any time, any place, but it is far too undignified to be stretched out on the carpet by a mere . . . by a female. All right, I accept that Miss Judith has learned some esoteric wrestling tricks in your godforsaken country, but as for the rest I never heard such a farrago of nonsense."

Giles shrugged. Jodie wondered whether to try to convince the earl of their veracity or just to persuade him to keep his mouth shut. In the silence, they heard the butler's voice in the hall.

"She's in the book room, Miss Emily, with Mr. Giles and Lord Thorncrest."

"Oh dear!" said Emily, and they heard her quick, light footsteps approaching. "Thank you, Potter. Bring refreshments, if you please."

The gentlemen rose and bowed as she entered. She took no notice of them but ran to hug Jodie.

"Is everything all right?" she whispered.

"Sort of." Jodie spoke aloud. "I'm afraid we aroused his lordship's suspicions and had to tell him our story. He didn't believe it though."

"Did not believe it?" Emily turned to her betrothed. "Surely, sir, you cannot suppose that they invented such an extraordinary tale?"

Looking harrassed, Lord Thorncrest ran his fingers through his dishevelled hair. His elegant cravat had also suffered. "To tell the truth, I don't know what to think, Emily. So you know of their claims?"

"I was there when they arrived from the future." Emily

calmly sat down on the sofa and motioned to the gentlemen to be seated. The earl took his place at her side. "Jodie, pray send for your book. That is the best evidence, I believe."

"Yes, of course. I'll fetch it."

Emily continued, "I was in the stables at Waterstock during a thunderstorm, Charles—never mind why."

Glancing back as she left the room, Jodie saw that Emily's cheeks were pinker than usual. She was perfectly composed though, and looked Thorncrest in the face as she went on with her description. He listened with eager attention.

He was listening to her, and he had called her Emily. What was more, she had boldly addressed him as Charles. Was it possible, Jodie wondered, hurrying up the stairs, that this idiotic situation might bring the pair together at last?

The book about Ada Lovelace was concealed at the bottom of a drawer. She carried it down half hidden in the folds of her skirt, though it was not too conspicuous as it had lost its dust jacket long since. Emily was right, it was the best possible proof of their story.

It was not needed. The earl stood as she entered and said awkwardly, "I beg your pardon for doubting your word, Miss Judith. Emily has persuaded me of the truth of your travels in time."

"Pray do not mention it, my lord," she said graciously. A glance at Giles's amused face told her that he had already received an apology. She held out the book. "Perhaps you would like to see this nonetheless?"

Thorncrest took it and examined it with interest. "A life of Byron's daughter," he exclaimed. "I don't suppose you would lend it to me?"

"No!" said Emily sharply. He looked at her in surprise, frowning. "Believe me, Charles, it is best that you do not read it. It is unwise to seek to know the future. I have given a great deal of thought to the subject, these past weeks, and I am quite sure."

As the earl gazed down into her pleading face, his frown cleared and he nodded. He turned back to Jodie and gave her the book, then sat down again beside Emily. He took her hand and smiled at her.

"For now, I'll trust you, though sometime I shall want to hear your reasons. I cannot deny that I am disappointed to lose such an opportunity."

Her answering smile was shy. "If you want to learn about Jodie and Giles's time, there can be no harm in that. It is so far in the future, we shall all be long gone."

"Does that thought not disturb you?" he asked seriously.

Jodie decided it was time to stop eavesdropping. She leaned on the arm of the chair next to Giles and said, "Boy, am I glad you came home when you did. I wondered how many times I'd have to toss him before he got the picture."

"It's been a most amusing morning, after starting off badly. Harry's been delayed by floods. Cassandra's naturally a bit cagy on the subject, but I gather he hasn't the funds to put in proper drainage and some of his tenants' farms are under water. It's your wretched year without a summer, I suppose."

"Don't blame me. It would be raining even if I hadn't told you. I wish we could do something for them, they are doing so much for us."

"I might as well be penniless for all the use my money is to me here, or to anyone else. I can hardly borrow from Roland to give to Harry, even if he would accept it."

"How frustrating! I'll keep trying to think of some way to help them."

"I have the utmost faith in your ultimate success. There's no such word as failure in your lexicon."

She wrinkled her nose at him, grinning. "Flattery will get you everywhere, kind sir."

At that moment Potter ushered in two footmen and a maid, all bearing refreshments.

"I took the liberty of having Cook make up some sandwiches, Miss Emily," he said, "thinking as the gentlemen might be sharp-set."

"Thank you, Potter. I do not know about the gentlemen but I am positively ravenous."

Jodie was delighted. If Emily was willing to admit to an unladylike appetite in Thorncrest's presence, she must be feeling very much more at home with him. He served her himself from the buffet set up on the desk, asking her preference in a way that suggested a desire to please rather than mere politeness.

Since Jodie had just eaten breakfast, her lack of appetite was genuine, not ladylike pretense. She accepted a cup of tea from a teasingly solicitous Giles, and sipped it while she answered the earl's questions about her own time.

He was fascinated, but at last he turned to Emily and said soberly, "I can see that you are right. It is best that we do not know too clearly what is to come."

"Not beyond tomorrow evening, at least," she responded. "Do you go to the Duke of Devonshire's ball?"

"Only if I may hope to see you there. As we are betrothed, I believe it will be permissible for me to claim three dances, will it not?"

Blushing, Emily granted his three dances. He looked warily at Jodie.

"Dare I ask you to stand up with me, Miss Jodie?"

She laughed. "I shall not throw you across the floor, if that is what you mean. Nor am I offended that you did not believe . . . Oh drat, that sounds like Roland out there. Where did I put that book?"

They all put down their plates hurriedly and started searching. In the hall, Roland's voice rose to a squeak of annoyance.

" . . . Eating in my book . . . Lord Thorncrest is here? Oh, very well. But really, we have a perfectly good dining room." The door began to open.

"Here." Emily pounced on the book, lying on the lower level of a tiered table.

Giles grabbed it and sat on it. Retrieving his plate, he took a quick mouthful and started to choke. Jodie wasn't sure if he was pretending, to distract attention from their flustered state, or whether, if he really was choking, she should apply the Heimlich maneuver.

Lord Thorncrest dashed over and pounded him on the back, with unnecessary enthusiasm in Jodie's opinion. She hastened to the rescue, bearing a glass of ale. Roland entered to a scene of total confusion, in which only his sister appeared to be sane.

The earl leaned towards Jodie over Giles's head and whispered, "I take it Faringdale knows nothing?"

"No. You will not tell?"

"If I did, I'd end up in Bedlam," he said sardonically, "which may be where all of us belong."

$== 14 ==$

CHARLOTTE PUSHED AWAY her dish of bottled plums. "I wish strawberries were in season," she said.

"It will be at least two or three months before even the Cornish strawberries are ripe," Roland pointed out from the far end of the dinner table. "It is not like you to wish for the impossible, my dear."

Catching Charlotte's eye, Jodie told him, "Preg—ladies who are in the family way often have odd fancies. My mother says the only time she ever ate yogurt was when she was expecting."

"Yogurt? Ah, a Red Indian dish, I daresay." Pleased with his own acumen, Roland turned back to his wife. "My love, if there is anything I can obtain for you, you know I will spare no expense, but how to come by strawberries in March I cannot guess."

"No, I know it is impossible," Charlotte sighed. "They would have to be grown in hothouses, no doubt. Giles, did you not mention that your friend Lord Font means to experiment with growing luxury crops out of season in greenhouses?"

"He has spoken of it." Giles looked suspiciously at Jodie, who put on an air of saintly innocence. "He hopes to do for market gardening what some fellow in Norfolk has done for farming."

"Coke of Holkham?" Roland was nibbling at the bait. "I have put many of his admirable ideas into practice at Waterstock."

"I knew you were interested in modern ideas," Jodie

flattered him, "ever since Giles was so fascinated by your experimental lightning rod."

Emily added her mite. "Roland takes after Papa."

"Yes, of course, your bathroom fixtures. It must be pleasant to be in a position to support useful innovations."

"Just think," said Charlotte, sounding wistful, "if Lord Font had started his enterprise some time since, perhaps I could have had strawberries today."

Giles picked up his cue like a professional. "Unfortunately Harry's short of capital. I'm afraid it'll be a while before he can provide fruit out of season."

"Well, we can't have that," Roland said jovially. "I want a large family and if it takes fresh strawberries in March to make you happy, my dear, then that's what you shall have. I'll have to see about investing in this scheme of Font's so that I may have a say in which crops he tries first."

Jodie tried hard not to look too triumphant.

After dinner, in the few minutes before the gentlemen joined them in the drawing room, the ladies congratulated each other on the success of their plot.

"I shall invite Lord Font to dine," Charlotte decided. "And Mrs. Brown too, of course. I have been thinking for some time that I ought to call on her. Will you go tomorrow to introduce us, Jodie?"

Jodie agreed as Giles and Roland came in. Giles had not adopted the habit of drinking port or brandy after dinner but he always sat with his ancestor. He had told Jodie that Roland only took a very small glass of port, often leaving half of it. He suspected Roland did not care for the taste and was just keeping up appearances.

Giles went to the piano and began to play an idle tune. Jodie followed him. Leaning against the instrument, she grinned at him smugly.

"*I* never told Charlotte about Harry's plans," he said, shaking his head in mock reproof.

"No, I did."

"Conspiracy."

"It worked, didn't it?"

"The poor chap didn't stand a chance. I'm glad Harry will

be helped but I must admit to some fellow-feeling for my gullible forefather. A matter of masculine solidarity."

"I know what you mean. It's a lousy way to go about it, but in this day and age, and with someone like Roland, it's really the only way. He had to think it was his own idea, and Charlotte knows just how to go about it."

"Taking advantage of his affection for her."

"It's not the way I'd choose to operate." She shrugged. "What else is she to do? It would be great if she could tell him, 'Look, this guy's helped your great-grandson, he needs a hand, and besides it may be a good investment.' But she can't, and it's not just that Roland is a male chauvinist pig."

"Hush," Giles warned, playing louder.

Jodie realized her voice had been rising with her passion. She went on in a soft and reasonable tone. "I can understand how inheriting the title and all that responsibility when he was just out of school could make him obsessed with proving his authority, and at least he's managed to stay kind and loving. But the whole society is run by and for MCPs. Jeez, I thought it was bad back home! I'm warning you, if we have to stay here I'm going to turn into a raving feminist."

"I can see the transformation beginning. Believe me, I understand your feelings, but do try to keep them under control until we find out whether we can go home. I wish Harry was not stuck in the Kentish mud."

"Don't worry, I'll keep my cool, as long as I can let off steam to you now and then. You'll know if we can go as soon as Harry gets here, will you?"

"We have to compare calculations. That should tell us the whether, then we have to work out the how."

"Charlotte means to call on Cassandra tomorrow and invite her and Harry to dinner."

"Whatever I said about her methods, my great-grandmother is a sweetheart."

"Isn't she? I only wish I could be certain that she really will be your great-grandmother."

They both looked across the room at Charlotte. She had every bit of the bloom tradition ascribed to mothers-to-be, pink cheeks, sparkling eyes, and a cheerful smile as she bent over the tiny garment she was sewing. Even the fair curls peeking out from under her lacy cap gleamed with health. It was hard to believe that anything could go wrong, but Jodie's thoughts flew to Ada Byron's ignorant doctors thirty years hence, and to Princess Charlotte's death in childbed next year.

"I don't like that Dr. Croft," she said decisively. "I shall see if Cassandra can recommend someone better to Charlotte. It wouldn't surprise me if when Cassandra decided to stay here she looked around for a doctor who would at least be willing to adopt twentieth-century notions of hygiene."

"An excellent idea," Giles applauded. He started to play in earnest and drifted away on a tide of music.

As she watched and listened, it dawned on Jodie that she loved him.

His fingers moved over the ivory keys with a touch at once strong and delicate, incisive and tender and impassioned. Jodie shivered. She wanted to feel his hands on her skin. Yet there was more to it than desire. She loved the way he lost himself in what he was doing, whether science or music. His face was dreamy, his blue eyes focussed on an inner vision, his lips—better not to dwell on his lips.

It was hard to believe that only last night those hands had wielded a deadly sword with consummate skill. Back to back they had fought for their lives. That was a bond of friendship that could never be broken.

Nor had he felt his manhood diminished by her ability. She loved him for respecting her intelligence, for listening to her ideas, and taking her seriously even when he disagreed. Admittedly those virtues were thrown into strong relief in contrast to the world they found themselves in. Still, Brad had wanted her to give up her scholarship because he could not go with her. She could not imagine Giles demanding such a sacrifice.

Oh boy, she thought, *I must really be in love if I can't see any faults in the man. This is dangerous.*

"Cousin Judith, will you take a hand at pinochle?" Roland requested playfully. "Learning your colonial game has quite destroyed my pleasure in whist, I declare."

"I should be sorry to think I had destroyed anyone's pleasure," she said, glad of the interruption. She joined the others at the card table.

When she went up to her chamber later, Jodie found her book on the bedside table.

"Mr. Giles gave it to me," Dinah told her, thrusting a warming pan into her bed. "He said not to let the chambermaid see, as if I would. Not that she'd know it were any different, being an ignorant girl. A book's a book, for all she knows. There, that'll warm your toes nicely, miss."

"Thank you, Dinah."

"My Miss Emily seems right perky tonight. I reckon as something good's come her way this day?" the abigail hinted.

"She was able to set Lord Thorncrest right on a couple of points," Jodie obligingly revealed. "They are coming to a better understanding, I believe."

"Ah, men's the very devil, begging your pardon, miss. That Frederick for one." Dinah giggled. She did not look in the least as if she wished to consign the footman to hell. "Can I ask you something, miss?"

"Go ahead."

"Where you come from, would a lady's dresser be lowering herself if she walked out with a footman? A right smart footman as'll be butler some day," she added quickly.

Jodie was perplexed. She tried to think of the nearest equivalents: a beautician and a waiter? Not really—but she was losing sight of her democratic ideals.

"Lower herself? Heavens no. But can you marry and keep your places?"

"Lor, miss, I'm not thinking to wed yet awhile. 'Sides, I 'spect Miss Emily'll want me to go with her when she's my lady Thorncrest."

"I am quite sure she will."

"I s'pose she might ask his lordship to take Frederick too, but there's no knowing, is there? If we was to end up in the same household, why then'll be time enough to think on weddings. If there's naught else I can do for you, Miss Jodie,

I'll be off to see Miss Emily's comf'table. And thank you, miss, for advising me."

Jodie hoped her advice had been sound. She could recite the ranks of the peerage in order of status, but she was much less sure of the lower classes' pecking order. It was all double-Dutch to a Southern Californian anyway. She wondered how much of the caste system was still around in modern England, whether it would be a shocking *mésalliance* for a viscount to marry the daughter of an American lawyer and a half-Chinese biology professor.

Whoa, there! she scolded herself. There was no reason to suppose Giles felt anything but a sense of responsibility towards her. No, he did like her at least. He probably saw her as the younger sister she was pretending to be, a frequently irritating younger sister.

Brother and sister—no hope of anything more if they were stuck here in the past. Jodie wanted to go home.

Self-pity would do her no good. She reached for her book. Her place was still marked, with Cassandra's first letter, the one announcing her presence in 1816. Cassandra had given up her time and her career for Harry Font's sake. From what little Jodie had seen of them together they seemed a well-matched pair, unlike Lord Byron and Annabella Milbanke.

In the short time that the latter couple had lived together, the prim, scholarly miss and the libertine poet who referred to her as his "Princess of Parallelograms" had made each other absolutely miserable. At this very moment, Annabella was busy destroying her husband's reputation and beginning the long years of self-justification.

Their daughter and Lord Lovelace had started out well. It was impossible to guess how much Lovelace's increasingly stodgy, stingy personality had contributed to Ada's unfaithfulness and gambling debts. A need for excitement inherited from her father was partly to blame, and the primitive medicine of the day that prescribed laudanum for all ills.

Jodie read on. Her candle was guttering when at last she put down the biography with a sigh.

A horrible death, with her mother dinning into her that

her suffering was payment for her sins—what a dreadful end for the little girl now sleeping peacefully no doubt at her grandmother's Kirkby Mallory estate in Leicestershire. An unnecessary death in twentieth-century terms, and if Ada had lived in the twentieth century, what might she not have done with her mathematical talents?

The candle flickered out. Jodie fell asleep with that question in her mind and the warm, sweet scent of burning wax in her nostrils.

The next morning, the three Faringdale ladies called at Lady Bestor's little house in Dover Street. Cassandra welcomed them with slightly surprised pleasure.

"I haven't quite got the hang of this morning call business," she confessed to Jodie while Charlotte and Emily exchanged remarks on the weather with the aged aunt. "I guess it's something of an honour to have Lady Faringdale call on me?"

Jodie frowned in thought, then gave up. "Could be. American widow and rich viscountess. Charlotte's the dearest creature, though. I hope you'll want to keep in touch with her, and Emily, when—if Giles and I leave."

"They know about me?"

"Yes, and you can talk openly about it with Emily but go easy on Charlotte. She prefers not to think about it if she's not forced to. Emily's betrothed, Charles Thorncrest, had to be told, too."

"Jodie," Charlotte claimed her attention, "only think, Lady Bestor knew Lord Thorncrest when he was a child."

"And a naughty little boy he was too," said Aunt Tavie roundly. "Charming, withal, and a good-looking young devil. Still is, by what I hear."

"Have you met the earl, Mrs. Brown?" Charlotte enquired.

"No, ma'am. I do not go about much in Society," Cassandra admitted.

"I hope you have no rooted dislike for company, ma'am. Lord Faringdale and I hoped you and Lord Font might join us for dinner one evening."

"A family party," Emily added. "Do come."

"Thank you, I shall be delighted. I cannot speak for Lord Font, though. He is not in town at present."

"We shall wait until he comes to arrange a date," Charlotte assured her. "Lady Bestor, may I beg you to honour us with your presence also?"

"Prettily said, young woman," Aunt Tavie replied. "However, I generally fall asleep round about the time you modern fashionables dine. In my youth it was dinner at three, you know, and none of these skimpy three courses neither. Nine courses was thought a decent dinner. I remember the roast peacocks at the Squire's, and tureens full of syllabub."

Charlotte and Emily gave their attention to the old lady's reminiscences or inventions. Jodie turned back to Cassandra.

"I'm hoping you can help me," she said. "Charlotte's breeding—pregnant, I mean."

"I'm not a medical doctor, I'm afraid."

"I know. I just wondered whether you've found someone here who's half-way competent. Charlotte's seen Dr. Croft. He's very well thought of but I don't trust him."

Cassandra hesitated. "There is a man, Witten his name is. He's a friend of Harry's cousin Tom. I've taught him a bit about hygiene, and using nitrous oxide for anesthesia, not that I know much. He's willing to learn. The trouble is— well, he has a drinking problem. He's good if you manage to catch him sober but he's just as likely to be in a stupor."

"Sh-drat, that doesn't sound too great."

"It's post-traumatic stress syndrome. He was in the Peninsula with Wellington's army. Not that that's any comfort to a patient when his hands start shaking." She shrugged. "The best I can say is that I'll keep an eye on Lady Faringdale and do what I can for her. I'd worry most about childbed-fever, and I expect one could find a midwife who could be persuaded, or bribed, to be particularly careful about cleanliness."

"Thank you, I can't ask for more. Or rather, I can. There's something else I'd like to know."

"Shoot."

"I hope you don't say that to Harry! This is my question: What do you think would happen if a person from this time travelled to the future?"

"I don't know." Cassandra frowned. "Unfortunately, Giles has pointed out a few flaws in the law of Conservation of Reality, and Harry tends to agree with him. I haven't had a chance to work on it—I guess I never will, now. If you'd asked me a month ago I'd have said nothing would happen, according to both the math and to my own experience. Now I have to say it depends. No more satisfactory than my doctor, I'm afraid."

"It'll do," said Jodie optimistically.

Charlotte chose that moment to take their leave. Cassandra accompanied them into the entrance hall.

"You are not expecting Lord Font today, I collect," Jodie said to her as the footman opened the front door.

"Not today. He writes that he intends to come tomorrow without fail."

"He writes to you daily?"

Cassandra nodded, blushing. Jodie was prepared to wager that Dr. Brown of MIT hadn't known how to blush before she took up residence in the past.

As the three young ladies settled in the barouche, Charlotte said guiltily, "Oh dear, I do not know what Lady Bestor must think of me. We stayed far too long for a morning call. Only I could see that you wanted to talk to Mrs. Brown, Jodie, and it must be such a comfort to her to know a female who understands her situation. I did not want to interrupt."

Jodie decided she agreed with Cassandra, she simply did not understand the etiquette of morning calls. If one found congenial company it made no sense to limit one's visit to a polite quarter of an hour.

"And then," Charlotte went on with a roguish look at her sister-in-law, "Emily started to question Lady Bestor about Lord Thorncrest's childhood. Naturally it was impossible to leave until all had been discovered."

Emily blushed. "I believe her ladyship did not object to my questions," she said defensively.

"Tell me everything she said," Jodie ordered.

The recital lasted until they reached home. A message awaited them there that brought further blushes to Emily's cheeks. Lord Thorncrest begged pardon for the short notice, but would the Faringdales do him the honour of dining at his house that very evening, before the Duke of Devonshire's ball.

It was the first time the earl had issued an invitation. Jodie had no hesitation in ascribing it to his new-found respect for his betrothed. She envied Emily, though she had decided long since that dashing, handsome, macho Lord Thorncrest was not what she wanted. An arranged marriage might have its drawbacks but undeniably it added a certain sense of security to the courting process, a security Jodie was far from feeling in any aspect of her life.

At least, since Harry was still in Kent, Giles had no excuse not to go with them to the ball at Devonshire House.

== 15 ==

"I'M GLAD TO SEE you're not wearing your livery to this affair," said Giles as Jodie joined him in the living room. "A ball gown suits you much better."

"I only hope all the gossipmongers do not recognize it." The amber silk had been retrimmed with knots of rich brown velvet ribbon. "Charlotte wanted to buy me a new one but I simply could not accept it. Sometimes I think she has forgotten that I am not really your sister, that I have no possible claim on her and Roland."

"I know what you mean, even though I am distantly related. Fortunately a gentleman is not expected to turn out in a new coat for every occasion."

"You are prodigious elegant in black and white. Do you ever wear a tux at home?"

"A dinner jacket? As rarely as possible. You should see me in my robes for the state opening of Parliament."

"You mean you get all dressed up in red velvet and ermine and parade around the House of Lords? Oh Giles, not a coronet?"

"I'm afraid so."

"Now that I have to see to believe." She giggled.

"I've only done it a couple of times, but I go up now and then to speak on scientific matters. I wear a white lab coat; it seems to impress people."

"You constantly surprise me. I did not know you had any interest in government."

"*Noblesse oblige.* Given a free soapbox, I feel it's my duty to stand on it occasionally. Roland's the same, I may say.

134

He'd rather steer clear of the place and tend his acres. However," he added, deliberately sententious, "we Faringdales have duty bred in the bone."

"And pomposity," Jodie snorted. "It's Roland's besetting sin. If it wasn't for that, his other faults might be easier to overlook, because he's not a bad guy in lots of ways."

"I shall endeavour to overcome my inherited tendency to pomposity," said Giles solemnly.

"Idiot. I never met anyone less pompous in my life."

The others came in and they all set off for Lord Thorncrest's house. Emily was wearing deep rose with a white lace overdress. Jodie thought she had never seen her look so happy and carry herself with such confidence. It was amazing what simply having her opinion consulted had done for her, and all because the earl had recognized Jodie in the Royal Saloon.

His lordship came out to his vestibule to greet them, and escorted them to the drawing room. To Jodie's surprise, he had also invited a number of his own relatives, all appearing perfectly respectable. His younger brother and his wife, both plump and cheerful, welcomed Emily with open arms. There were also an aunt and uncle, and their daughter with her husband, all amiable if uninteresting.

Emily met them with composure and joined in the conversation, which centered around Princess Charlotte's coming marriage to Prince Leopold. Though Lord Thorncrest listened with a cynical air to the romantic raptures of the ladies, Jodie noticed that more than once he cast a glance of approval toward Emily. To Jodie, his attitude could only be described as wary.

After a few minutes, he took Emily aside and spoke to her privately and briefly. She colored, hesitated for a moment, then nodded, whereupon he took her hand and led her back to the group. There was an expectant hush.

Thorncrest cleared his throat and tugged at his neckband with an uncharacteristic uncertainty. "Most of you know, or have guessed," he began, "that Miss Emily and I have been unofficially engaged for some weeks. I wish to announce that she has done me the honour of agreeing to make the betrothal official. A notice will be sent to the papers immediately."

There was some applause and a great deal of kissing and congratulating, and then they went in to dinner.

Emily was seated at the earl's right hand and Jodie was some way down the table, but she watched the couple whenever she could spare attention from her neighbours. To her exasperation, she saw that Emily had returned to her bashful reticence. Lord Thorncrest helped her to the most delicate morsels with evident solicitude, but then he had never treated her with less than courtesy since Jodie had known them. She wondered whether his attitude had really changed.

Most of the party were not going on to Devonshire House. Rather than fit a sixth person into the Faringdales' carriage, thus endangering the ladies' gowns, Thorncrest suggested that he should take up Emily.

Emily looked alarmed, and Charlotte a trifle worried, but Roland considered it a most suitable notion which settled the matter.

"Don't worry, he can't eat you," Jodie whispered to Emily, squeezing her hand. "If he misbehaves, remind him that *I* shall await him at Devonshire House."

Emily managed a feeble giggle.

In fact, it was she and the earl who arrived first, as Roland's coachman had settled comfortably in the Thorncrest kitchens and had to be routed out. When Jodie reached the ballroom of the vast mansion on Piccadilly, they were among the dozens of couples already on the floor. Fortunately, Giles managed to find the four of them seats near the set in which Emily and Lord Thorncrest were dancing.

"Oh dear, what has gone wrong?" Charlotte said to her softly. "I thought Emily was quite comfortable with him, but they are as stiff as marionettes."

"I don't know," said Jodie, frowning, "but you may be assured that I mean to find out."

The dance ended. The earl brought his woebegone partner to join her family. He looked puzzled.

It was hardly possible to embark upon an interrogation in the ballroom, but to Jodie's surprise he abruptly asked her to stand up with him for the next set.

"All right—I mean, thank you, my lord, that will be delightful. Only let us not dance. I want to talk to you."

Again the wary look entered his eyes, but he said grimly, "Precisely my own desire. Pray take my arm, Miss Judith, and we shall find somewhere less crowded. However," he added, "I am not going anywhere with you unless you wipe that scowl off your face."

Jodie forced her lips into a bright smile. Charlotte was anxiously whispering to Emily. Giles and Roland—typical men!—apparently had no idea anything was amiss. She took Thorncrest's arm and they made their way around the ballroom.

There were several anterooms. They decided the card room was the most appropriate for their purpose, inhabited as it was by matrons playing silver loo and gentlemen of all ages with more serious games in mind. There were a number of small tables set up for piquet players, and at one of these Lord Thorncrest seated Jodie.

A footman brought cards and another offered a tray of champagne-filled glasses. The earl accepted both.

"A game of piquet, Miss Judith," he asked politely, setting one glass before her.

"I do not want a drink and I cannot play piquet."

"Pretend. We cannot sit here doing nothing, and I refuse to play pinochle in public. It will only arouse attention. I shan't dun you for my winnings." He removed a number of cards from the pack, shuffled and began to deal.

She glared at him. "What did you do to Emily?" she demanded.

"Nothing." He shrugged helplessly. "That is, nothing but ask her to allow me to publish a notice of our engagement. She agreed, as you know."

"You did not try to kiss her in the carriage?"

"I do not go about forcing my attentions on defenceless fe . . ." He flushed. "Well, you were not precisely defenceless. Pick up your cards and pretend to be interested."

137

She obeyed. "So you did not kiss her. Perhaps you should have."

"For heavens sake, Jodie!" he said in exasperation. He put down four cards face up and picked up four from the pile on the table. "I mean, Miss Judith. How could I kiss a girl who shrank into a corner and when I spoke to her would only murmur 'Yes, my lord,' and 'No, my lord.' It's your play."

"She just suddenly clammed up, huh?" Jodie laid down four cards at random.

"Yes. No, you can only discard three unless you want one of those I discarded."

"How the hell do I know whether I want one? I haven't a clue what I'm doing. Okay, okay, I'll take that one. She must suddenly have gotten nervous when you brought her to the point."

"I have twenty-three points. I have sometimes wondered whether Faringdale forced Emily to accept me."

"In the first place, yes. Here, you count up my points for me. But lately I have thought she was reconciled to the marriage."

"You are flattering! Your hand is worth twenty-nine. Are you sure you have never played before?"

"Never. All right, better than reconciled. She was beginning to quite like the idea. She was terrified of you at first, you know. That was why she was hiding in the stables in a thunderstorm."

"Tricks," said Lord Thorncrest blankly, as if he had suddenly lost his train of thought, or one of them. "Terrified? You cannot trick me so easily—I was not even at Waterstock that night."

"Tricks? We play for tricks? Don't be muttonheaded, Thorncrest, she wasn't hiding from you, just hiding her misery from her brother."

He played a card and stared silently at the one she put on top of it.

"Did I take it?" she asked, reaching for them.

"No, it's mine. But if she was becoming reconciled, why has she turned shy as bedamned again? I don't want a terrified wife. That one's yours."

"I don't know." Jodie picked up the trick and played a card. "I'll have to talk to her."

"I did not really want a wife at all, yet I too am growing reconciled to the notion. There is a lot more to Emily than I had guessed. Pretty, complaisant, well-born, wealthy—I knew all that before I approached Faringdale. But she's intelligent, too." He sounded surprised. "She has a mind of her own, and besides, there is something about her. . . . Dash it, Miss Judith, you have gone and taken all the tricks while I was rambling on!"

"I daresay that means I have won?" asked Jodie, smugly pleased not only with the game but with the tenor of their conversation. Lord Thorncrest was at last beginning to appreciate Emily as he ought.

"Yes. A *partie* usually consists of six games, but I must get back to Emily. We did not settle on stakes. I usually play for pound points, so I'll give you a draft on my bank."

"Don't be muttonheaded, we were not playing for money. I haven't a penny in this world."

"I beg your pardon, I had forgotten your circumstances, though that only makes it the more reasonable that you should accept your winnings."

She shook her head, adamant.

"Very well, but I hope that as my wife's cousin you will always feel you can turn to me in case of need." He paused. "Sweet-natured—that is the word I was looking for."

Jodie was touched. Perhaps the earl might make a good husband for Emily after all.

"Actually," she said, "picquet is not that different from pinochle."

When they returned to the ballroom, Roland was just leading his sister into a waltz. Giles jumped up from Charlotte's side.

"Charles, if you will keep my cousin company, Jodie has promised this dance to me."

Thorncrest looked somewhat disconcerted, but accepted with good grace what he could not escape without being ungentlemanly. Giles whirled Jodie onto the floor.

"What's going on?" he demanded. "Charlotte wanted a private word with Thorncrest and Emily looks like the middle of a wet week."

"It *is* the middle of a wet week," Jodie pointed out. "I daresay it is some stupid misunderstanding. Emily has turned missish again ever since Thorncrest asked permission to announce the engagement."

"Perhaps you should toss him around a bit more."

"I don't think it's anything he has done. He claims innocence and he seems pretty upset. Maybe Charlotte can sort it all out. Talking about it isn't going to help, unless you have some startling revelation?"

"No startling revelations, I'm afraid. Do you have any good tidbits about our host, as you did at the Cowpers'?"

"The Duke of Devonshire? Lord, yes. At least, the present duke merely fell in love first with Caro Lamb and then with Princess Charlotte. Two narrow escapes. He will never marry though, probably because of the trauma of the household he was brought up in."

"That bad?"

"A classic *ménage à trois*," Jodie told him. "The present duchess—Charlotte says she lives abroad—was both the last duke's mistress and best friend of the last duchess, Georgiana, our host's mother. They all lived together for decades, while Georgiana ran up enormous gambling debts, like Ada Lovelace actually only on a grand scale. When Georgiana died the duke married his mistress, so she's the present duke's stepmother, if you follow me."

"I think so."

"And Byron is renting a house belonging to the duchess but he hasn't paid the rent and the bailiffs will arrive ten minutes after he flees."

"How do you know all this?" asked Giles curiously.

"Most of today's on-dits will end up in tomorrow's books. There's even one called *The Scandalmonger*. After all, scandal is one of the chief pastimes of the age."

"Which gives you every excuse to study it. It is in our time too, of course, only most people are more interested in film stars than the aristocracy."

"How fortunate for you," Jodie teased, curtsying as the music ended. The waltz had gone by far too fast. She regretted having talked instead of concentrating on the pleasure of being in his arms.

"Save the next waltz for me," he requested. "I wouldn't want you to miss it and you know how Roland dislikes you dancing such a shocking dance with strangers. Speaking of strangers, here comes a dear friend of yours."

"A friend?" Jodie turned to look, and groaned. "Lord Alfred Barnes! Save me, Giles."

"Too late, he's seen us. Good evening, my lord."

"Evening, Faringdale. Miss Judith, beg you'll do me the honour of standing up with me." The young man's round, beaming face was ingenuous, but Jodie remembered his love of cockfighting and ratting—and that he had described her as a spirited filly.

Not to mention the soaking she had received on the back of his carriage.

On the spur of the moment she could think of no valid excuse to refuse. With a despairing moue at Giles, she took Lord Alfred's arm. Another memory returned—bruised toes.

"I am quite out of breath after waltzing," she invented rapidly. "Shall we walk about instead of dancing?"

"Just as well," he confessed. "I'm none too sure of the steps of the country dances. Perhaps you will like to take a breath of air on the terrace?"

Jodie agreed, for despite its size the room was crowded and stuffy. However, when they reached the French doors they found them firmly closed, with rain streaming down the panes.

"Dash it," said Lord Alfred. "Let us try the conservatory."

As they turned away, Emily reached the end of the set nearest them. Jodie saw that she was dancing with the young duke, which must mean that Thorncrest had not yet managed to talk to her.

Lord Alfred followed her gaze. "That's your cousin, ain't it? Heard she's caught Thorncrest. And he don't mean to whistle her fortune down the wind, I can tell you, for all he's no need of it. Saw him with my own eyes last night paying off his fancy piece, and heard her squeal, deuced if I didn't."

"He did?" asked Jodie as they entered the green dimness of the conservatory. Red and blue and yellow patches of light cast by a few Chinese lanterns left deep shadows between. Over the babble of voices and music from the ballroom came the sound of rain drumming on the glass roof.

"In the lobby at Drury Lane." His lordship continued to stroll between the potted palms and towering ferns. Here and there, on discreetly placed benches, couples whispered and giggled. A whiff of orange blossom made Jodie intensely homesick for a moment. "She's an actress," Lord Alfred went on. "Pretty wench, won't have any trouble finding a new protector, but she knows which side her bread's buttered, I reckon."

"She does?" asked Jodie, fascinated.

"Stands to reason. Thorncrest can afford to be generous to his ladybirds and he don't stint 'em, I'll say that for him though he's a nasty way with his tongue sometimes. He gave the jade a diamond bracelet, and I'll go bail they were real. Course she knew what it meant and let out a shriek you could hear a mile. Ah, here we are."

He pulled Jodie down on a vacant bench and pressed his lips to hers.

Taken by surprise, Jodie's first thought was that Lord Alfred hadn't had much experience kissing. Next she wondered whether to let out a shriek you could hear a mile or to toss him into the ornamental fountain she could see over his shoulder. And then she realized that either expedient would inevitably lead to an unnecessary fuss and a lot of awkward questions.

Lord Alfred's free hand, the one that wasn't clutching her arms to her sides, was beginning to wander. What the hell was she supposed to do?

$=16=$

GILES GRINNED AS he watched Jodie walk off on Lord Alfred's arm. Her memories of the youthful gentleman were evidently none too fond. She would probably read him a lecture on the inhumanity of cock-fighting.

He made his way around the room towards Charlotte, intending to ask her if she would care for a glass of lemonade. Roland was with her, beaming with satisfaction as their host, the Duke of Devonshire, led Emily onto the floor. He was an attractive young man with a look of gentleness much more suited to Emily than Charles Thorncrest's acerbic nature. It was a pity, Giles mused, that history said the duke never married. To encourage a prominent historical figure as a suitor for his great-aunt would cause appalling paradoxes.

A hand on his arm made him look round. It was Thorncrest.

"Your sister's gone into the conservatory with young Barnes," he said. "He can't be trusted to hold the line. You'd best go after them."

"You of all people should know that she can take care of herself."

He flushed slightly. "Not here, not without creating a scandal. If you will not go, I shall. I don't want my future wife's cousin the talk of the tattlemongers."

"I'll go with you." Giles sighed as he wondered how Jodie had managed to get into trouble at a thoroughly unexceptionable ball.

They strolled with outward casualness to the conservatory. After the brightness of a thousand candles in glittering chandeliers, Giles's eyes took a moment to adjust to the shadowy, multi-coloured dimness.

"The devil!" murmured Thorncrest. "We'll never find them in here." He led the way into the humid, plant-smelling gloom.

It was less difficult than they feared. There was enough light to see that every female, whether locked in an embrace or merely whispering in her beau's attentive ear, wore curls or ringlets. Thank heaven, Giles thought, for Jodie's recalcitrant hair.

They found the pair near the fountain. Jodie was clasped in the young man's arms, her one visible eye reflecting redly the light of the nearest lantern. It signalled wildly an appeal for help.

Giles and Thorncrest approached side by side. They each grasped one of Lord Alfred's arms. Taken by surprise he loosed his hold on Jodie and squeaked as they bodily lifted him from the marble bench.

Lord Thorncrest's hand promptly covered his mouth. "Keep your mouth shut," he warned grimly. He turned to Giles. "I told you she would give this cawker the wrong impression, going off into the conservatory with him."

"We were just talking," said Jodie, her voice low despite her evident indignation, "and then he attacked me."

"Just talking!" snorted Lord Alfred. "I was telling her how you gave your light-o'-love the brush-off, Thorncrest. She never tried to stop me. She was even asking questions. If that ain't fast I'd like to know what is."

"You told her about that scene last night?" The earl sounded shocked. He turned to Jodie and asked urgently, "Does Emily know that I had a mistress in keeping?"

"I don't know. She wouldn't have talked about it if she did."

"You see?" said Lord Alfred, injured. "Respectable females don't discuss the muslin company. Young unmarried ones, at any rate."

He stepped backwards in alarm as both gentlemen turned on him.

"Do shut up," said Giles mildly.

"You stay out of this," ordered the earl. "Jodie, are you going to tell Emily I gave the girl her marching orders?"

"Heavens no. She's a respectable female. I might shock her." Not unnaturally, Jodie sounded sarcastic.

"But I want her to know. Please tell her."

"Coward. Tell her yourself."

"Women!" said Lord Alfred in disgust. To Giles's relief he took himself off.

Jodie said seriously, "I mean it, Thorncrest. If she's going to be your wife till death do you part, it's about time you stopped being afraid to communicate with her."

Even in the dimness of the conservatory Giles saw the earl's anger at her insult begin to change to thoughtfulness. However, he merely said with asperity, "Giles, do try to persuade your sister to conduct herself with a little more concern for the proprieties." He followed Lord Alfred back to the ballroom.

"That was a bit of sage twentieth-century advice you hit him with," Giles observed, laughing.

"Men!" she said bitterly.

Giles took her hand and sat down, tugging her after him. She subsided unwillingly.

"You're overwrought, Jodie. Sit still for a minute. Quiet now. Take a deep breath."

She obeyed and her hand relaxed in his, her frazzled nerves calming. "When that toad started to paw me I didn't know what to do," she confessed. "The fountain made a tempting target but we'd never have been able to explain how he landed in it."

"No, you were quite right. You have Charles to thank for your rescue. It never dawned on me that you might be in difficulties."

"That's because you're a normal person." She slid closer on the bench until her side was pressed against his, her thigh warm through the thin silk of her gown. "You're the only man I can talk to without being afraid that something I say or do is going to be regarded as an invitation to assault. Oh Giles, I want to go home!"

After what she had just said, it was hardly the moment

to take her in his arms and kiss her troubles away. He had to content himself with patting her knee and saying with brotherly sympathy, "I hope it won't be long now."

It was too much to expect him to go on sitting there with her warmth pervading him, her fragrance in his nostrils. He stood up and looked down at her.

"Let me see if you're fit to appear in public. We can't have Roland wondering what's become of you."

Docile, she rose and faced him, slender and lithe and altogether desirable in her shimmering silks. No wonder neither Thorncrest nor Barnes had been able to keep their hands off her! Giles tucked a stray strand of black hair under a braided coil and offered his arm. The words of a song learned in childhood returned to him.

"Madam, will you walk?"

She put her hand lightly on his arm and they returned to the ballroom.

Though it seemed to Jodie that an age had passed, Emily was still dancing with the duke. Or rather, they stood waiting while another couple skipped down the set. The duke said something that made Emily laugh. Lord Thorncrest was glowering them from the side of the room, his arms folded, every inch the Byronic hero.

Jodie had long since reached the conclusion that Byronic heroes were much overrated, but a little bit of jealousy might be a good sign.

"Stop scowling," she hissed, as she and Giles passed him. "You will scare her to death."

His grin was rueful. "It seems I am never to speak to her. A ball is not the best place for private conversation."

"Take her to the card room," Jodie suggested, "or better yet, the conservatory."

Since Emily did not return to Charlotte's side before the next dance began, Jodie assumed the earl had taken her advice. Her own partners kept her occupied for the next hour, so she had no chance to talk to Emily before supper was announced. At that point, Roland decided that Charlotte was tired. He offered to take her home and return to fetch the others, but they were all ready to leave. Jodie had found it a singularly exhausting evening.

Nonetheless, she had no intention of going to sleep without finding out what, if anything, had happened between Emily and her betrothed. She waited impatiently for the household to settle.

At last the last door closed, the last servant plodded up to the garrets. Jodie was bracing herself to leave the warmth of her bed when there came a light knock at her chamber door.

"Jodie? Are you awake?" A candle appeared round the door, followed by Emily in her nightgown and frilly nightcap.

"Yes. Come in and stick your feet under my covers before you get frostbitten toes. The Romans had central heating; I cannot imagine why you don't."

"Perhaps because they had cheap wood to burn and we have expensive sea-coal."

"You are too logical, my dear. That was a complaint, not a question."

"I believe some houses are heated by circulating hot water from a boiler. No doubt Roland will have it installed one of these days."

"No doubt, but you did not come here to talk about central heating."

"I do not know where to begin."

"At the beginning. Why did you retreat to your shell when Thorncrest wanted to announce your betrothal?"

"Oh dear, you make me sound like a frightened snail."

"You are not still frightened of him, are you? I thought you were reconciled to marrying him."

"I was. I am. Oh Jodie, I feel like such a ninnyhammer," Emily wailed. "It was all because he asked my permission to put a notice in the papers, instead of arranging it with Roland and then telling me."

"What was?" Jodie asked patiently.

Emily fixed her gaze on her clenched hands. "I realized that I am in love with him."

"But that's splendid!"

"And I cannot bear it, because he is a rake, and he kissed you, and he has mistresses. I am shockingly jealous."

"He kissed me before it really dawned on him what a treasure you are. And did he not tell you tonight about casting off his mistress? I told him to take you into the conservatory and confess all."

"He did. He said all sorts of kind and flattering things, and promised he means to be a good husband. But I know even married men take mistresses. They say Lord Byron has an actress *and* Miss Clairmont now, even though he is shattered that his wife has left him."

"People keep telling me respectable unmarried young ladies do not know about such things! There are many faithful husbands, Emily. Can you imagine Roland being unfaithful to Charlotte?"

"No, but Charles is more like Lord Byron than Roland, and besides, Roland loves Charlotte."

"Just because Charles has not said that he loves you, it doesn't mean that he doesn't. Lots of men have trouble saying it. Actions speak louder than words."

Emily's lips quivered. "I know. When he took me into the conservatory I was sure he was going to kiss me, but he didn't." She burst into tears. "He kissed you," she sobbed, "and all those loose women, but he didn't kiss me. If he doesn't like me *that way*, what does it matter if he respects me?"

Jodie reached over to grab a handkerchief from the bedside table, then took the weeping girl in her arms and rocked her. "He didn't want to shock you," she said. "You are a proper young lady."

"B-but we are betrothed. It w-would not have been so very imp-proper, and besides, there was no one to see. If he loved me, he would have kissed me."

A number of answers flitted through Jodie's mind. Lord Thorncrest might have a greater sense of propriety than they gave him credit for. He might have been afraid of his own desire, of displaying a passion that must frighten a gently-bred girl. But perhaps Emily was right—he simply did not care for her in that way.

While Jodie hesitated, unsure whether to suggest possibilities that might mislead her, Emily took the handkerchief and blew her nose.

"I know it is too much to expect that he should love me," she said bravely. "I am sure he will be a kind and considerate husband and it is gooseish of me to hope for more. Thank you for listening to my megrims, Jodie." Kissing Jodie's cheek, she slipped out of bed, pattered across the floor and was gone.

Too late, Jodie thought of a thousand words of comfort and advice. Perhaps it was just as well she had no chance to utter them. Confused herself, she was in no position to advise Emily. After all, Jodie had sat in the privacy of that same dark conservatory with Giles, and he had not kissed her.

How easy it would be to tell Emily to communicate her feelings to Charles Thorncrest. Yet Jodie had no intention of telling Giles she loved him, not until she had some inkling whether he returned her feelings.

=== 17 ===

THE MEN IN JODIE'S and Emily's lives were notable by their absence the next morning. Giles had received a note informing him of Harry Font's arrival in town late last night and he had gone off early to Dover Street, bearing a dinner invitation from Charlotte. Lord Thorncrest, who might have been expected to call the morning after requesting a formal betrothal, did not turn up.

Chaperoned by Charlotte, Jodie and Emily listlessly entertained those gentlemen who did have the manners to pay a courtesy call after dancing with them at the ball. While these included the Duke of Devonshire, to Jodie's relief, Lord Alfred Barnes was not among them.

Lady Bestor's footman brought an acceptance from Cassandra and Harry.

"For tonight," Charlotte exclaimed, hurriedly folding her needlework. "I left the choice of day to them, and it seems Lord Font is taking Mrs. Brown and Lady Bestor down to Font Hall tomorrow. Oh dear, we are uneven numbers. I shall invite Lord Thorncrest."

"Pray do not," Emily begged. "If he does not choose to visit, I would not have him imagine I care."

"Nonsense, he is your betrothed, not a suitor. He is the only person who knows the whole, and as he is soon to be one of the family he will not be offended by the short notice. I hope," she added optimistically.

"Shall I write the invitation for you?" Jodie offered. "Then he will just regard the lack of proper notice as one of my peculiarities."

"Yes, please do. I must speak to Cook at once. Poor Mrs. Brown is such a very long way from home, I want everything to be just right for her."

Charlotte went off happily about her domestic duties. Jodie wrote a note to Lord Thorncrest and sent Frederick out with it. The footman returned an hour later to report that the earl was not at home and not at his club, and his people did not know where else he might be found.

"So I left the message at his lordship's house, miss," he concluded.

That meant that Thorncrest still might accept the invitation, so Charlotte could not ask anyone else to balance her table. She began to look flustered.

"I promise Cassandra will think nothing of it," Jodie soothed her. "It is not important in our time. Besides, it will be much more comfortable tonight if there are only people who know about us."

"Roland does not," Charlotte pointed out. "Heavens, are Mrs. Brown and Lord Font aware of that?"

"I am not sure. You are right, that could be awkward," Jodie agreed. "I had best send Frederick to Dover Street with a note to Giles."

Not until after five did Lord Thorncrest's footman appear with an acceptance. The earl himself arrived at a quarter past seven, when everyone was dressing for dinner. Frederick ran upstairs and passed on to Dinah a request that Miss Emily would grant his lordship a few minutes of private conversation before the arrival of the other guests.

Emily rushed to Jodie's chamber. "He wants to cry off!" she wailed.

"Fustian. He wants to apologize for not calling this morning."

"I am not dressed yet."

"Then you will just have to keep him waiting until you are."

"I cannot see him alone. Pray go with me."

"I shall bring Charlotte to rescue you precisely five minutes after you go down. Off you go now and dress."

With Dinah and Matty scurrying backwards and forwards

from bedchamber to dressing room and back, the three ladies were all ready in short order. They met at the head of the stairs. Emily was pale, but otherwise pretty as ever in her favourite cowslip-yellow with a gold locket about her neck.

"Five minutes," promised Charlotte.

"Honestly, you would think she was going to the guillotine," Jodie said as they watched her descend to the hall.

"I put his lordship in the book room," they heard Potter say in a fatherly tone, "being as he wanted a private word with you, Miss Emily."

With one nervous backward glance, Emily disappeared from sight.

"I suppose we cannot go and listen at the door," Jodie sighed.

"Gracious no," said Charlotte, shocked, then she giggled. "At least, not with Potter waiting in the hall."

Precisely five minutes later the rescuers marched down the stairs and into the book room. Emily and Thorncrest, standing by the fireplace, turned towards them. Jodie was relieved to see that Emily's face was alight with pleasure.

"Look!" she cried, putting one hand to her throat. "Look what Charles has given me."

Her locket had been replaced with a double strand of pearls alternating with tiny gold beads, from which depended a gold filigree flower with pearl petals and a cabochon-cut yellow stone twinkling in the center.

"I had the very deuce of a time finding a yellow star sapphire," the earl explained his absence as Charlotte and Jodie exclaimed over the necklace. "Diamonds are too hard and glittering for Emily, and topaz too common. And when I found it I did not care for the setting." He put his hand in his pocket and drew forth two small, velvet-covered boxes. "Lady Faringdale, Miss Judith, I hope you will accept these small tokens as a remembrance of our betrothal."

While they were trying on the identical rings, set with seed pearls, Roland and Giles came in.

Roland voiced his approbation. "I call that very handsome of you, Thorncrest. There's nothing like a little jewellery to please the ladies."

Jodie caught a fleeting look of guilt crossing the earl's face and she recalled that, according to Lord Alfred, he had paid off his inamorata with a diamond bracelet. Still, he had undoubtedly gone to much more trouble over Emily's gift. She had no intention of giving him away.

Cassandra and Harry arrived a few minutes later. Over dinner, the talk was mostly of their plans for experimental market-gardening. Unexpectedly, Lord Thorncrest was enthusiastic.

"Three of my tenants grow soft fruit and vegetables for the London market," he said.

Jodie was surprised that he even knew what his tenants grew, let alone took an interest in it. She was beginning to like the man, and to think him almost worthy of Emily.

As the ladies were withdrawing at the end of the meal, Roland said jovially to Harry, "If you don't mind talking business over your port, I should like to discuss the possibility of investing in your scheme."

Cassandra at once returned to the table. "I'll stay then," she said, resuming her seat.

Jodie turned back to watch the drama.

Roland was thoroughly disconcerted. "Business, ma'am," he spluttered.

"Mrs. Brown is my partner as well as my future wife," said Harry, looking harassed.

"In that case," Lord Thorncrest put in smoothly, "we shall certainly want to hear her views. I too am interested in investing."

"Hear her . . . but . . . Ah, I had forgot, Mrs. Brown is an American lady." Roland managed to back down gracefully. He was to be further tried.

Emily stepped forward and said in a small but determined voice, "I should like to stay also."

Lord Thorncrest pulled out the chair beside him. "Of course, my dear. After all," he said to Roland, a hint of malice in his tone, "Emily is *my* future wife and I value her opinion."

Roland's mouth opened and closed twice without a sound emerging. Charlotte seized Jodie's hand and fled.

"I *could* not let him think I too wanted to join in," she was explaining to Jodie when Giles followed them into the drawing room.

"Very wise," he said, looking gloomy.

"What is wrong?" Jodie asked.

"Wrong? Nothing. I just find it depressing that a first-rate physicist is in there discussing the cultivation of asparagus and cucumbers." He slouched over to the piano and began to play moodily.

Jodie agreed. It was almost as depressing as that a talented mathematician, Ada Lovelace, should waste her abilities on an unappreciative nineteenth century and die young of a preventable disease.

She knew that Giles was also worrying that he might yet find himself abandoning physics for farming. He had told her when he came home to change for dinner that the outcome of their calculations was not yet certain. A few hours more would give them the answer. In fact, they could have reached it tonight had they not decided that Charlotte's invitation must take precedence. Jodie was glad Roland intended to invest in Harry's enterprise. Nonetheless, she could not help wishing the three scientists had stayed with their equations until they could tell her whether she would ever see her home again.

She forced herself to listen with sympathy to Charlotte's delight at having done Mrs. Brown and Lord Font a good turn.

Giles went early to Dover Street the next day. Jodie was restless with anticipation. She did not want to leave the house in case she was out when he came back, but she could settle to no occupation. When Charlotte and Emily went out to pay some morning calls, she decided to keep her fingers busy by tidying Charlotte's work-basket, no easy task as it was already in apple-pie order.

Fortunately Giles returned before she had reorganized it in such a logical arrangement that Charlotte would never be able to find her favourite needle.

"We've done it," he said nonchalantly, entering the parlour with a jaunty stride.

"Done it? We can go home?" Jodie squealed, and flung herself into his arms. "When?" she demanded as they danced a sort of jig around the furniture.

He deposited her in a chair and dropped into the one opposite. "I'm not absolutely sure yet. The final calculations won't take long but we have to build a battery with the right voltage, collect all the equipment, and get it all to Waterstock. I'll have to go down to Font Hall with Harry and Cassandra and Aunt Tavie."

"They're going today, aren't they?"

"This afternoon.. They're going to be married on Easter Monday. I'm hoping we'll be gone by then."

"Yes, we don't want to intrude on newly-weds. Today's Saturday. That gives us nine days?"

"At most. I'll write from Font as soon as I know what's what. I must go and pack now."

Taking Dinah, Jodie went with him to Dover Street to say goodbye to Cassandra, in case she did not see her again. Despite her obvious joy at her coming wedding, the physicist's reserve almost broke down on taking leave of the only woman who truly understood what she was giving up. Once again Jodie was sorry she had not made more effort to befriend Cassandra.

They stood on the pavement, watching Harry help Aunt Tavie into her huge, resplendent travelling carriage. Painted blue with red and gold trim, it was emblazoned with a coat of arms and pulled by six horses.

"I know you have no family at home," Jodie said. "If you ever come back, for any reason, you must call me. Here, I wrote down my parents' phone number and I'll tell them about you. They'll always know how to get in touch with me and if there is anything I can do to help, you have only to ask. We'd have been stuck without you."

"I don't have a quarter for a phone call." Cassandra smiled though her eyes were bright with unshed tears.

"Ten p. in this country, but call collect. Reverse charges, rather. I'll tell Mom and Dad to accept the call."

"Bless you."

They hugged each other as Harry turned to collect his

bride. Jodie saw the tenderness in his eyes.

"He loves you," she whispered.

Would Charles Thorncrest ever look that way at Emily? Would she ever see that expression in Giles's eyes, meant for her alone?

"You should hear from me by Tuesday, Jodie," he said, following Harry into the carriage. "Don't get into too much trouble while I'm gone. Cassandra, just how much difference do you think the precise latitude and longitude will make?"

Reminded of the career Cassandra was abandoning, Jodie stuck her head in at the window. "Giles, I want to take Ada Byron with us."

"Impossible. Harry, we mustn't forget to take your sextant and chronometer."

As the heavy coach rumbled away, Jodie was very much tempted to thumb her nose at it in the contemporary gesture of scorn.

When she and Dinah reached Grosvenor Street, Charlotte and Emily had just returned. They were pleased that she was going to be able to go home, sad at the prospect of losing her. A few tears were shed, interrupted by the footman bringing in an invitation.

"At least you will have one more party before you go," Charlotte said, reading the engraved card. "Lady Jersey and Madame de Lieven are holding a private assembly at Almack's on Monday."

"Is that April 8th?" Jodie asked. "I would not miss it for the world. At last I shall see Lord Byron."

"Oh no, I doubt he will go. They say he does not go out in public for fear of the hissing of the mob."

"He will be there," said Emily. "Jodie knows what will happen, do you not, Jodie?"

"Yes, but I shall not tell you. Nothing too shocking, I promise you."

"Do not tell Roland that Lord Byron will be there," Emily advised, "or he will probably decide we should not go."

Jodie kept to herself the fact that the unhappy poet's scandalous half-sister was also going to be present.

The assembly rooms in King Street were already crowded with chattering fashionables when the Faringdales and Lord Thorncrest arrived. By now Jodie could put names to many of them and she saw that most of the leaders of the Ton were there. It was kind of Lady Jersey to go to such an effort to rehabilitate Lord Byron.

Whatever the gentlemen and matrons were gossiping about, it was Princess Charlotte's romantic betrothal to Prince Leopold that as usual occupied the tongues of the young ladies. Jodie could not join in, knowing that eighteen months hence the popular heir to the throne would die in childbed. She found herself constantly glancing worriedly at the princess's namesake, wishing she had reminded Cassandra of her promise to keep an eye on Charlotte's pregnancy.

Seated some distance away with Roland, Charlotte too seemed worried, her glance flying to the door at each new arrival. Jodie realized she was anticipating Byron's appearance and wondering what on earth to do when he came.

If Lady Jersey's party was designed to still slanderous tongues, in one sense it succeeded. The poet's entrance, with his sister at his side, was greeted with dead silence. The crowd parted before them as they approached their hostesses, Byron limping with thunderous face, Augusta Leigh holding her flaming cheeks high in proud defiance. As they passed, ladies turned away their heads, snubbing Augusta with cruel deliberation. People began to drift towards the other rooms.

Though she had known what was coming, Jodie was incensed by their pitiless condemnation. She laid her hand on Lord Thorncrest's arm.

"Introduce me," she demanded fiercely.

He looked uneasy. "I am not well acquainted with Mrs. Leigh," he evaded.

"Then introduce me to Lord Byron. He is your friend, is he not? You *cannot* add to his shame by ignoring him."

"Very well, if you insist." He gave in to her determination. "Emily, I'll take you to your brother."

"No, I shall go with you." Emily's quiet determination equalled Jodie's.

Thorncrest frowned. "My friend or no, George is no longer an acceptable acquaintance for a young lady. Miss Judith is soon to depart. You will still be here for the cats to sharpen their tongues upon."

"As my future husband's friend, his lordship must always be an acceptable acquaintance to me."

"I can see I am taking a managing wife," the earl complained, but he was smiling down at Emily. "As you will. I daresay I shall in any case be blamed for the whole."

Lord Byron was leaning against the mantel at the far end of the no longer crowded room. As they approached him Jodie felt disapproving eyes upon her. Nonetheless, they were not quite the only ones to brave censure to speak to him.

A short, red-haired young lady was fluttering her eyelashes at the glowering outcast. "You had better have married me," she said. "I would have managed you better."

When he failed to respond she turned away, undismayed.

"Miss Mercer Elphinstone," Thorncrest whispered to Jodie. "She may be right. George, let me make you acquainted with the Misses Faringdale. Miss Judith is a visitor from America, and her cousin Miss Emily is my betrothed."

Lord Byron bowed. "Charles cannot fail to make you happier than I ever made Annabella," he said gloomily to Emily.

Jodie asked him about his travel plans, and they stood for a few minutes discussing his itinerary as if it were to be a journey of pleasure, not a permanent exile. The poet summoned up a pallid enthusiasm when he spoke of Greece, but it was a relief when Lady Jersey came up and they could escape without giving offense.

Though Jodie was not sure whether she had been right to insist on the introduction, she was proud of Emily for her support—even if she had done nothing but clutch Charles's arm and gaze upon Lord Byron in wide-eyed silence. Judging by the way he pressed her hand, Charles was proud of her too.

He really was not such a bad fellow when you came to

know him. Tomorrow, Jodie decided, she would ask him to lend a hand in her project to rescue Byron's daughter and take her into the future.

=== 18 ===

A LETTER FRANKED BY Lord Font awaited Jodie at the breakfast table on Tuesday. Charlotte had not yet come down and Roland had already gone out, so only Emily watched with bated breath as Jodie slit the seal and scanned Giles's neat writing.

"Saturday," she said. She reached for her coffee cup and swallowed a gulp. "We go home Saturday. I cannot believe it. I feel as if I had always lived here."

"So do I," said Emily sadly. "I wish you had, except that you would then not be you. I wish . . . No, I am glad for your sake that you are going back to your own family and your own life. What more does Giles say?"

"He and Harry will need to spend Friday setting up and checking the equipment. They will be here Wednesday night—tomorrow already!—and we shall drive down to Waterstock on Thursday in Lady Bestor's coach."

"What are you going to tell Roland? How fortunate that he went out early today."

"Giles has it all figured out. We have received a message from America saying we are urgently needed at home. Urgent! Well, I suppose in today's terms two or three months can be considered urgent. Our return passage is booked on the ship that brought the news, which will depart from Bristol on Saturday morning."

Emily looked dubious. "The servants at Waterstock are bound to mention your being there with the scientific equipment."

"He is going to ask Roland's permission for Harry to go

there after he leaves us at Bristol, to do some experiments with the lightning rods. With any luck, Roland will just think the servants confused if they happen to mention that we were there too." She pushed her empty plate away. "I'm not hungry. Let's go and tell Charlotte."

Charlotte was sitting up in bed with her tea and toast, her blonde curls escaping from beneath a delightfully frivolous lace nightcap. She shed a few tears on hearing that the date of Jodie's departure was fixed, but she approved the explanation for Roland and promised to smooth over any questions that might arise.

"Only I daresay he will want to lend you our carriage," she added anxiously, "and then he will know exactly where you went."

How well she knew her husband, Jodie marvelled, as Roland swallowed the story hook, line and sinker and went on to insist that he would not hear of them borrowing a stranger's coach. By then, Charlotte had an answer ready.

"Lady Bestor is a very aged lady, dear," she told him. "She has taken a fancy to Cousin Giles and will be mortally offended if he rejects her aid."

With a fond smile, he patted her hand. "You are so very considerate of the feelings of others, my dear. Naturally we shall do nothing to distress the old lady. I shall content myself with giving Giles money for the post charges."

Knowing something of the state of Harry's pockets, Jodie was glad to accept.

She waited impatiently for Lord Thorncrest to come to take Emily driving in the park. Though she had no idea how she was going to accomplish it, she was determined to take Ada Byron home with her. Of course there would be problems when she arrived with a little girl, but she would face those when she came to them. In the meantime, with Lord Thorncrest's help surely she could find a way to remove the child from her sanctimonious, overbearing mother.

When Lord Thorncrest heard that she was leaving soon, he willingly agreed to take her up for one last turn about the park. He refused, however, to leave Emily behind so he sent his curricle home and they took the Faringdales' barouche. Unfortunately, that meant Roland's coachman was sitting up in front with his ears wide open.

It was a rare sunny afternoon and the park was crowded with carriages, riders and pedestrians. Jodie hoped the coachman would be too preoccupied to concentrate on his passengers' conversation. The rumble of wheels and crunch of hooves on the gravel, and the voices of the Polite World greeting each other, would partially cover her voice. Nonetheless she spoke softly and tried to make her words innocuous.

"Thorncrest, I need your help. There is a child I want to adopt and take home with me."

He raised his devastating eyebrows, less than quelling now that she knew him. "Oh?"

"The daughter of a friend of yours. The parents are separated and the little girl is going to have a miserable life. I *know* she is."

"A friend we met last night?" he asked cautiously.

"That's right." Jodie was pleased with his quickness. "She is presently in the Midlands. I have only three days to make all the arrangements before we depart and I cannot do it without your assistance."

"You relieve me. You must be mad even to contemplate such a thing."

"I thought you were a dashing out-and-outer, up to every rig and row," she said indignantly.

"A dashing out-and-outer, possibly. A kidnapper, no. Are you sure you are warm enough, Emily? The breeze is quite chilly."

Jodie accepted the rejection with no good grace. She racked her brains but could not figure out how to reach Leicestershire, let alone rescue Ada, without help. Kidnapper indeed, she fumed. Her aim was not to abduct the child but to save her from a wasted life and painful death.

For the rest of the day she had little chance to think about the problem. Roland and Charlotte were determined to spare no effort to entertain her. After a long evening at the theatre, she fell asleep as soon as her head touched the pillow.

* * *

Emily woke Jodie, gently shaking her shoulder. She blinked up sleepily at her friend then sat up in alarm.

"What's wrong? Is that from Giles?" She took the paper Emily held out to her.

"No, from Charles, under cover to me, and he says it is urgent. I cannot think what it is about." Emily settled comfortably on the bed as Dinah came in with a jug of hot water.

Jodie unfolded the note. "He saw Lord Byron last night, dining at the Clarendon with friends. It seems he is distraught at the prospect of leaving England without seeing his daughter once more."

"The poor man. He did look very unhappy Monday night."

"Thorncrest says he thinks my notion of taking Ada to the future is an air dream—huh! He does, does he? But if I am willing to take care of her, and if I can be ready to leave by noon, he will drive me to Kirkby Mallory and help me kidnap her. I wish he would not use that word!"

"I cannot believe he means to do anything so shocking." Emily was horrified.

"Lady Byron will make Ada's life miserable," Jodie reminded her. "And . . ."

"No. Do not tell me more. What does Charles intend to do once you have her?"

"He will take us to Waterstock to meet Giles. He is sure I shall not succeed in taking Ada with me, so then he wants to bring her back to London to see her father, before returning her to her mother. Well, we shall see about that." Jodie bounced out of bed, full of energy. "I must send him an answer and be ready packed to leave at midday."

"I shall go with you."

"Emily, you can't!"

"Why not? I think you are both fit for Bedlam, but you will need a chaperone. Roland will never let you go alone with Charles."

"Nor will he consider you a fitting chaperone."

"We shall take Dinah."

"Ooh, miss," squeaked the abigail, "we'll all be transported."

Emily ignored her. "Of course we cannot tell him we are

going into Leicestershire. Try to think of something that will satisfy him. Dinah, pray fetch our portmanteaux."

"His lordship'll never believe as Miss Jodie's going all the way to America with a couple of portmanteaux, miss."

"You are right. Have Frederick bring a trunk down. We shall put some of my things in it and leave it at Waterstock. I must go and see Charlotte."

"Don't tell her about Ada," Jodie said, "it will only upset her. Tell her I want to go back to Waterstock early to finish up some research."

"All right, but we cannot tell Roland that. As Dinah pointed out, he thinks you are going back to America."

"I know, we'll say I mentioned to Lord Thorncrest yesterday that I am disappointed not to see the home of my ancestors once more. He realized that by leaving today I would have time to go via Waterstock and meet Giles in Bristol on Friday."

"He has offered you the use of his carriage," Emily took up the tale, "He will escort you, and you wish to accept if I can go with you."

"He'll have to stay at an inn in Thame while we are at Waterstock, for propriety's sake, or Roland will have a fit."

"On Friday night in Bristol we shall be under Cousin Giles's protection, though."

"And on Saturday, when Giles and I sail, Charles will rush you back to London. That is a very long day's journey, is it not?"

"Yes, but I shall not regard it, because I am anxious to spend every possible moment with you before you leave."

"You are a splendid conspirator, Emily."

"That last bit is true. Charlotte and I are going to miss you excessively." Emily gave Jodie a quick hug and slipped from the room to go and tell her sister-in-law the version of their plans tailored for her.

Jodie wrote a note to Giles, to await his return that evening, and sent Frederick off with another for Lord Thorncrest. Emily came back just as she finished dressing and they went together to tackle Roland in his study. He accepted their story with such complaisance that Jodie wondered if he wasn't just a trifle relieved to be getting rid of her.

She was ashamed of her suspicion when he said kindly, "I know how very attached you two have grown. It is a sad thing to part from friends with little hope of meeting again."

Much to his embarrassment, Jodie kissed his cheek. "It is your generosity that has enabled us to become friends. We can never thank you enough, cousin."

"Yes, well, head of the family and all that, you know," he muttered, red-faced, and patted her hand. "You have done a splendid job of learning to fit in with English Society's little foibles. At first I was quite concerned—but no matter. Your visit has been a pleasure, Cousin Judith."

Jodie heard a little snort from Emily and was hard put to it to keep a straight face. If Roland had even an inkling of her less respectable activities in London—but he didn't, thank heaven.

With a return to his fussy manner, he was giving his sister instructions. "Though you are betrothed, you must have a care to your reputation, Emily. On the journey back from Bristol, Thorncrest must escort the coach on horseback, not travel within. I shall speak to him. Keep Dinah with you at all times, and if you should have to stop overnight en route, which I trust will not happen, she is to sleep in your chamber. I am glad, my dear, that you are willing to entrust yourself to Thorncrest, but remember that you are not yet wed."

Emily blushed. "Yes, Roland," she said meekly.

"I should not let you go if I did not know that you are a good girl," he added with a benevolent air.

That was a statement guaranteed to produce guilt, if ever Jodie had heard one. She hurried Emily out of the room and on the way upstairs kept her occupied with questions about what to pack for the journey.

Jodie's packing did not take long, consisting only of a change of clothes for the road, her sheaf of notes on the pastimes of Regency England, and the few odds and ends she had brought with her from the future. Among these was the biography of Ada Lovelace. Before she put it into the portmanteau, she flipped through the pages.

There was the portrait of Ada as a child; a bright, loving child but frightened of her mother, she would be glad to escape. She should not be too difficult to deal with, Jodie thought hopefully. Any qualms she felt she quickly suppressed as the book fell open at the sketch of Ada on her deathbed, drawn by her mother, the mother who had told her that her agony was fitting expiation for her sins.

Her determination reinforced, Jodie went to take her leave of Charlotte, who had just gone down to the parlour.

"It is hard to believe you have only been with us a month and a half," she said, holding Jodie's hand in both hers. "You have blown through our lives like a breath of fresh air."

"Why, how poetic, Charlotte. More like a gale, perhaps," Jodie said, laughing.

"Perhaps." Charlotte's blue eyes twinkled. "But you have changed things for the better. I wish you really were going to America, so that I could say with some hope, come back and see us again. I shall never forget you, Jodie."

"Nor I you. You could not have been kinder if I really were Roland's cousin. Though I had no intention of coming here, I have enjoyed it beyond anything. You will take care of yourself, will you not?"

At that moment Lord Thorncrest was ushered in, an impressive figure in his multi-caped greatcoat, whip in hand. Servants were scurrying about loading luggage onto his elegant midnight-blue chaise. Cook appeared with a luncheon hamper, which Jodie was very glad to see as she had forgotten breakfast.

There was no time now for more than formal farewells. Jodie, Emily and Dinah stepped into the carriage and they were off.

Some hours later, in the vestibule at Font Hall, Giles bid Cassandra farewell.

"Don't worry," he said. "Whatever happens I'll send Harry back to you in time for the wedding on Monday." He nearly added, "If you're quite sure you won't come with us." The loving glance she directed at Harry dissuaded him. "I wish you both very happy."

"Thank you, Giles. Give Jodie my love." Though it was her own choice to stay, she sounded wistful. Harry moved closer and took her hand.

"You won't lose my phone number?" Giles pressed her. "If ever you do come home, if you need a job or anything else, just ring me. Jodie and I are very much in your debt."

"I have her parents' number too. I won't lose them, but I don't expect to use them. This is my home now."

"Good-bye then. I hate to tear you away, Harry, but we'd better get going if we're to reach town before dark."

"Good-bye, and God speed." Cassandra went out with them and stood on the front steps, waving, as Aunt Tavie's ponderous carriage swayed into motion.

Giles and Harry anxiously checked the packaging around the Leyden jars. Huge as it was, the interior of the coach was crowded with equipment. They would have been more comfortable riding, but they wanted to be on hand this short leg of the journey to make sure everything was safe for the longer drive from London to Waterstock tomorrow.

After a few remarks about their final calculations, Harry fell silent. Despite the difficulty of reading his face in the dusk, Giles received the impression that he was nerving himself to say something. At last it burst out, a torrent of doubts as to whether it was possible for Cassandra to be content with this unscientific society, with a world where her own worth would be measured by her husband's, where all her training was good for nothing.

Setting aside his own doubts, Giles did his best to reassure his friend.

"After all," he concluded his arguments, "you know Cassandra has thought it out carefully and come to a reasoned conclusion. She knows what to expect and she's taken it into account—unlike Jodie, who never looks a consequence in the face until it bites her."

Harry had to laugh. "You are right, I have not forced Cassandra into an unconsidered decision. Thank you, and I beg your pardon for troubling you."

"Not at all, old chap," said Giles.

He hoped he had convinced Harry. He had not convinced

himself. Cassandra was an exceptional woman, highly intelligent, good-looking, amiable. She had been headed for an impressive career in her own world. On the other hand she was reserved, so self-sufficient she had been, by her own admission, close to no one there. Perhaps she really had found her niche here, with a man whose love filled her need.

How different she was from Jodie, he mused. No matter where she found herself, Jodie would involve herself with people, make friends, captivate the women and attract the men. Look at the way Roland had succumbed, gradually ceasing to notice the exuberance he had found obnoxious at first. And without the least intention of winning him over she had Charles Thorncrest eating out of her hand.

Giles suppressed a spark of jealousy. There was nothing designing about Jodie's charm and in that particular case it was Emily who would profit by it, as Charlotte would by Roland's mellowing. Jodie brightened lives wherever she went.

He'd wager that Fifi, the *fille de joie* at the Royal Saloon, remembered her with kindness though they'd exchanged no more than a smile and a word or two.

The short journey had passed unnoticed. With much whoa-ing from Aunt Tavie's coachman, the carriage pulled up in front of the house in Grosvenor Street.

"I shall pick you up at eight in the morning," Harry said as Giles stepped down. "You know where to find me in case of need—at my cousin's house in George Street."

"Right, we'll be ready at eight. See you then."

The clock in the hall said half past seven, just time to dress for dinner. Giles handed his hat and gloves to Frederick and unbuttoned his coat.

"Mr. Giles!" It was the butler. "Her ladyship asked me to give you this the moment you arrived."

Giles took the twist of paper from the silver salver, noting with misgiving that his name was scribbled in Jodie's handwriting. He unfolded it. It took a moment for the message to sink in, then he screwed the note into a ball and threw it violently across the hallway.

"Bloody hell, Jodie's really gone and done it this time!"

=== 19 ===

"OH DEAR," SAID Charlotte. "Oh dear, I had a feeling Emily was not telling me everything." With a frilly white wrap hurriedly cast on over her petticoat, she looked like a ruffled goose.

Giles poked moodily at the parlour fire. "Ever since we came here we have been so entangled in a web of fabrications that I suppose one more seemed like no great matter."

"Your situation made it necessary," Charlotte said soothingly, "and you can be sure that Jodie has the child's best interest at heart, however misguided her notions. She is acting out of pure chivalry."

"I know it." He smiled ruefully. "Nonetheless, it's left to me to extract her from this folly, and I'm not sure how to go about it. The surest way to catch them is to ride after them tonight, but once I reach them, if Thorncrest does not choose to turn around and drive to Waterstock then I shall have to hire a chaise. From what I have heard of hired carriages we might not reach Waterstock in time."

"I believe they are horrid," shuddered Charlotte, who had never been subjected to one. "Besides, what would become of Emily? She would be left alone either somewhere on the road with Lord Thorncrest or with Lord Font at Waterstock. I shall have to go with you to lend her countenance."

"Which means taking your carriage, which means making up yet another explanation for Roland," Giles groaned.

"Yes, and he will insist on going too, I fear. How we shall account for Jodie going north when you are supposed to sail from Bristol, I cannot imagine."

"That's easy. Being unfamiliar with English geography,

Jodie confused two ports and told Lord Thorncrest our ship is at Liverpool, which is where we claimed to have arrived, you may remember."

"Jodie will not like to be thought so ignorant."

"Serves her right," said Giles callously. "I need a map, though, to work out what we should do."

"There is a map-book in the book room."

By a stroke of luck, the shortest route from London to Liverpool passed not far from Kirkby Mallory. Giles and Charlotte were planning their story when Roland came into the book room.

He greeted Giles, then turned to Charlotte. "Not dressed yet, my dear?" he asked reproachfully.

"I heard that Giles was come and I wanted to tell him that Jodie has already left. Oh Roland, the most shocking thing has occurred."

"Fortunately my sister left me a letter. She has made the stupidest mistake. It seems she has told Thorncrest we are to leave from Liverpool."

"Liverpool! Then they have driven north?"

"I'm afraid so. Cousin Charlotte and I have been consulting a map. If they stayed at Waterstock overnight, as they intended, they will have gone north through Birmingham, whereas the shorter way from London is through Northampton. The roads converge at Stafford, however. The only chance is to waylay them there and dash back to Bristol." Giles could only hope that en route he would come up with an excuse for detouring to find the miscreants at Kirkby Mallory.

Before Roland could speak his mind, a considerably disturbed mind by the look of him, Charlotte distracted him.

"I shall go with Giles," she announced. "Emily will need a chaperone on the way home."

"But my dear, in your condition!"

"I am very well, Roland, and it will do me no good to stay here fretting. Our carriage is excessively comfortable, since you were so clever as to have it built with the most up-to-date springs. Indeed I shall come to no harm."

"Liverpool!" said Roland again, helplessly. "It is at least

two days journey. What can Emily and Thorncrest have been thinking of?"

"Young people in love are notorious for not thinking," Giles pointed out. It was no time to let Roland think either. He hurried on, "I must let Harry know of the change of plans. You agreed that he might go to Waterstock on the way home from Bristol, to experiment with your lightning rod. I hope you will be kind enough to let him go straight there now?"

"Yes, yes, of course. I shall write to my steward immediately directing that Lord Font be given every assistance, and you may send it to him with your own message. But Charlotte dear, do pray go and dress."

"At once, Roland," said Charlotte meekly.

She did go and dress, but in a travelling costume not an evening gown. She managed to convince Roland that it was his notion to go as far as St. Albans that night, in order to shorten the morrow's journey. By the time they finished dinner her efficient household had everything ready, the carriage was at the door, and off they went.

My lord and lady Faringdale, accompanied by coachman, footman, abigail, and a generous purse, travelled swiftly. With frequent changes of horses, they reached Northampton on Thursday in time for luncheon at the Red Dragon. Charlotte consented to lie down for half an hour, though she did not appear to feel the need. Giles was amazed at her stamina. While she rested, he and Roland strolled a little to stretch their legs and then went to the tap for a glass of ale. The tapster regaled them with tales of runaway couples who had passed through the inn on their way to Gretna Green.

When they pulled out of Northampton, Giles still had no idea how to explain to Roland why he wanted to turn aside from their road to go to Kirkby Mallory. Roland himself provided the answer.

He had grown increasingly uneasy since listening to the tapster's revelations, casting glances at Matty, the abigail, as if wondering whether to speak in her presence.

"That's all very well," he suddenly burst out, "but Emily and Thorncrest are not in love."

Charlotte looked as blank as Giles felt.

"Not in love?" she repeated in puzzlement.

"Giles said they did not consider the distance from Liverpool to London because they are in love, but they are not. Thorncrest simply wants a conformable wife and you may recall that Emily was set against the match at first. Indeed, I almost called it off. It cannot be expected that they should dote upon each other even though I *was* under the impression that she had come to see the wisdom of my choice."

"You *were* under the impression, Roland?" Charlotte picked out the salient phrase.

"It's my belief that my sister still objects to the match and that Judith is eloping to Gretna with Thorncrest in order to save Emily from him."

"Good lord, she's not so quixotic as to marry a man just to save . . ." Giles started.

Charlotte silenced him with a look. "She is excessively quixotic, as well you know, cousin."

"It was obvious from the start that Thorncrest admired Judith." Roland conveniently forgot any number of *contretemps.* "I had not realized that he was infatuated to such a degree as to run off with her. The only thing I cannot fathom is why Emily should go with them." He frowned in bafflement.

"Why, as chaperone of course," Charlotte assured him. "The dear girl would not want Jodie to be compromised when she was going to such lengths for her sake."

"Some accident might prevent the wedding and leave Jodie in the lurch," Giles pointed out, wondering why Charlotte was fostering the illusion of an elopement but willing to trust her judgment.

"Or Thorncrest might harbour less than honourable designs," Roland said darkly. "I knew him to have something of a rakish reputation, but I trusted that marriage would settle him. I was never so shocked in my life as when he presented our girls to Byron the other night. I begin to doubt that he will do for Emily, even if we succeed in preventing this mad start."

Giles saw by Charlotte's look of alarm that this was taking the matter further than she had reckoned.

"I expect there's some perfectly harmless explanation," he said. "We'll find that Jodie did muddle Bristol and Liverpool, and the others simply didn't take the distance into account. However, in case you're right, I'll make a point of asking at every stop whether Thorncrest's carriage has been noticed." Of course, he thought, that was what Charlotte had been getting at. It would give them the perfect excuse to turn off the turnpike and head for Kirkby Mallory.

She smiled at him. "Thank you, Giles, that will set my mind at rest. You will let Giles enquire, will you not, Roland dear? It would look very odd for Viscount Faringdale to be making such enquiries, whereas Cousin Giles will not be recognized."

She should have been a politician, Giles decided.

Roland's comment about Byron suggested another persuasive detail. The moment came to report to Roland that Lord Thorncrest's coachman had asked an ostler the way to the late Lord Wentworth's estate at Kirkby Mallory.

"Apparently the man also wanted to know whether Lady Byron is in residence. Her mother inherited the estate, I gather. The ostler's not sure if she's there or in London, but it seems to me that Thorncrest might have brought a message from Byron to his wife, or possibly to her mother. In any case, they've gone in that direction, so we'd better follow."

Roland was so confused by this additional complication that he made not the least demur.

The village of Kirkby Mallory was a mere hamlet and its only inn, the Crooked Sixpence, little more than a tavern. Fresh whitewash and newly blackened beams, together with the rosy glow of firelight through the windows in the dusk, suggested that the weary traveller might find a degree of comfort within. These particular weary travellers noticed nothing but the dark blue chaise drawn up to one side of the building.

"They are here," said Charlotte with a sigh of relief. "Whatever we find, I am not stirring another inch this day."

Giles flung open the carriage door, jumped down without waiting for the step, and strode into the inn. A plump man in a white apron bustled forward.

"How may I serve . . ." His voice died away as Giles held up his hand.

Cutting through the babble from the taproom on his left, a clear American voice, raised in indignation, floated from a half-open door at the back of the house. "But you *promised* to help."

"I must have been mad," came Lord Thorncrest's answer. "I cannot possibly allow Emily to be mixed up in this havey-cavey business."

It sounded as if Jodie's plans had gone awry. Grinning, Giles sauntered down the stone-flagged passage and pushed the door open. The scene that met his gaze wiped the grin from his face.

Jodie stood in front of a blazing fire, hands on hips, glaring down at the earl. He was seated beside Emily on a wooden settle, his arm protectively about her shoulders. And in Emily's arms was a baby.

"Hush, you will wake it," she said softly.

Giles groaned. Three startled faces turned towards him. Only the crackle of burning logs and the sound of his footsteps broke the silence as he stalked forward and dropped into a cane-bottomed chair across the hearth from the settle.

"So you've got her already. I only hope you can come up with a way to give her back."

Three mouths opened to answer him, to be forestalled by Roland and Charlotte's entrance. With a face like thunder, pale blue eyes popping, Roland took in the appalling sight of his sister with a babe in her arms and a man's arm about her.

"What," he demanded awfully, "is the meaning of this? You shall answer to me, Thorncrest."

"I think I shall faint," said Charlotte promptly.

Emily jumped up, thrust the baby at Thorncrest, and ran to support her sister-in-law to a chair. Roland started bellowing orders, shouting for the landlord to bring harts-horn and sal volatile and brandy. Dinah and Matty rushed in, followed by Frederick, a waiter, and a small child in a smocked pinafore who stood sucking its thumb and watching the confusion with wide-eyed fascination.

Giles took Emily's place on the settle beside Lord Thorncrest and the baby, and beckoned Jodie closer.

"We told Roland Jodie made a mistake and you're on the way to Liverpool," he said swiftly. "He then came to the conclusion that you two are eloping. Lord only knows what he thinks now. He'll soon realize the baby can't be Emily's, so I expect he'll decide it's yours, Jodie, and possibly that Charles is the father. We have to get rid of it quickly. Any ideas?"

"That's easy," said Jodie. "It's the landlady's."

"What! You mean you . . ."

"Can we postpone explanations," the earl requested testily. "The brat has soaked me to the skin."

Jodie went off into peals of slightly hysterical laughter. The baby at once began to wail. Noting Thorncrest's scowl, Giles swallowed his grin and scooped the shrieking infant from his arms.

"My sister's—my *other* sister's child has done that to me a couple of times," he said with sympathy. "Dinah! *Dinah!* Return this to its mother if you please."

Emerging from the pack around Charlotte, the abigail obliged.

"I'm going to change," grunted Lord Thorncrest.

Giles pulled Jodie down beside him on the settle in the earl's place. She looked distinctly unhappy, he noted with a rush of tenderness. He steeled himself to sternness.

"Well?"

"Well, you see, I was thinking of Ada as a little girl. In my book, there's a portrait and a great description of her at two or three. So when Emily pointed out that she is only four months old, we decided to practise with the landlady's baby. It screamed all the time I was holding it," she confessed.

"You can't imagine what a relief it is to me to discover you haven't kidnapped Ada yet."

"We haven't come up with a plan to get hold of her. The

people here say there are guards, in case her father tries to abduct her. When Thorncrest heard that he backed out."

"I'm astonished he ever contemplated helping you. Jodie, it won't do. Quite apart from the moral and legal implications, there's absolutely no knowing what might happen if we tried to take her with us to the future."

"Cassandra came here without changing anything," she said stubbornly.

"We can't be sure of that." He ran his fingers through his hair. "Besides, Cassandra is a very different case from Lord Byron's daughter. Ada has a well-documented history, and she affected our own time at least to the extent of having a computer language named after her. There would *have* to be some changes, and we can't tell where they'd lead."

"But the law of Conservation of Reality . . ."

". . . is of limited scope. It applies to small matters in which some mistake might have been made or consequences are minor. I can't explain the maths to you, but I assure you, messing with the timestream is not a good idea. Perhaps you'll believe me when I say I've given up all thought of publishing when we get home."

"Oh Giles, no!" The concern in her dark eyes suggested that she guessed how difficult that decision had been.

He took her hand. "I don't know if I'm right to tell you this—I meant to wait until just before we go, so that you would not worry in advance, and Harry said I should not tell you at all—Jodie, there's some danger involved in going back. The numbers and equipment are as good as we can make them, and we know that Cassandra did it safely. Still, there's no guarantee. All other objections aside, we have no right to subject Ada to that risk."

Her little hand tensed in his. "You mean, we might come out some other time or place? Or our atoms spread out across the galaxy, or another dimension?"

If the room had not been full of people, he would have taken her in his arms and kissed the fear away. Instead he merely nodded. "It's up to you. You can choose to stay here."

"But you are going."

Again he nodded. "There's too much calling me home."

Her lips trembled but she managed a smile. "So if I stay, it will be *you* who are questioned by the police about *my* disappearance."

"That will make a much less interesting story for the tabloids. Don't try to make a quick decision. You have a whole day to make up your mind. But if we're not at Waterstock by early Saturday it's going to be pretty difficult to find another opportunity."

"It's only sixty miles or so. Charles said we can do it easily."

"With him driving, perhaps. He may not agree to, now. And don't forget that Roland thinks we are aiming at Bristol, which must be a good hundred plus, cross-country."

"Oh dear, poor Roland," said Jodie guiltily. "And he is worried about Charlotte, too."

The crowd around Charlotte was dispersing, leaving their patient looking remarkably, not to say suspiciously, pink-cheeked and healthy. Lord Thorncrest returned to announce that he had asked the landlord to add several dishes to the dinner already ordered, which would be served at any moment. Charlotte, who was being urged by her husband to retire, declared that she was more in need of sustenance than repose. A short while later they were all seated around the white-clothed table at one side of the room, eating and drinking as if they were an ordinary family party travelling on some perfectly unexceptionable occasion.

It could not last, Giles knew, nor did it. As soon as the waiter had withdrawn, Roland began to fuss.

"I do not know where you have hidden the child, but . . ."

"We must discuss how Giles and Miss Judith are to reach Bristol in time for their ship's departure," said Lord Thorncrest firmly.

"Impossible." Roland was diverted as intended.

"I think not," the earl said languidly, "if I drive. I am considered something of a whip, I believe."

"We must try," Giles said, with a grateful glance at Thorncrest. "Our passage is booked and it may not be easy to find another berth at this season."

"I shall go too," announced Emily. "I cannot bear to part with Jodie a moment before I must."

Roland was not about to let his sister out of his sight again without a fight. Once more Charlotte sprang to the rescue.

"Of course, if you think it necessary we shall go with them to chaperone Emily, but I confess I should prefer a day of rest before setting out again."

"I can easily return Emily to Waterstock instead of London on Saturday," Thorncrest proposed. "Then you can meet us there."

Roland was persuaded to agree to this plan. Giles noticed that Jodie did not join in the discussion. She had scarcely spoken to him since he had frustrated her charitable project, he realized with a pang.

The poor girl looked exhausted, pale with dark smudges under her eyes. Immediately after the meal she retired to the chamber the three ladies would have to share, and the others were not far behind her. The mythical need to reach Bristol next day dictated an early start.

Jodie twisted and turned on the uncomfortable truckle bed. What a mess she had made of everything! Giles must think her a complete nodcock. He had every reason to despise her.

When he had talked of the moral and legal implications of her plan to kidnap Ada, she had been ready to sink. Kidnap was the right word, she acknowledged. Knowing that Ada's life would be miserable gave her no right to interfere, to remove the child from her mother, her family, her world. There was no certainty even that she would have been happier or more fulfilled in the future.

No wonder, then, that Giles's decision to dare the dangerous way home did not depend on hers to go with him. If she chose to stay here she might do so with his blessing. Though her absence from the future might be a nine days' wonder, it would cause him little trouble. With no motive and no corpus delicti he could not be charged with murder. Her disappearance would grieve her family; to Giles she would be no more than a troublesome acquaintance he had parted from in unusual circumstances.

Tears welled in Jodie's eyes. She wiped them away and suppressed a sob, for in the big bed next to her Charlotte and Emily breathed evenly in the depths of tranquil sleep.

=== 20 ===

The sun had not yet risen when the little group of travellers stood outside the Crooked Sixpence next morning. While Roland issued a stream of commands to Emily, Jodie bade Charlotte another hurried good-bye.

"I'm sorry to leave you all alone here with Roland," she said, "but you will be back with Emily again tomorrow."

"I do not mind being alone with him," Charlotte protested softly. "He never scolds me any more since you came."

"In comparison to me, you are a veritable saint." Jodie's smile was wry.

"Oh no, just different. So different that I daresay you will not understand how it is that I love him. But I do, Jodie."

"I'm glad. I'm very glad."

They hugged each other wordlessly. Then Roland kissed Jodie's cheek and handed her into the carriage. As she settled herself beside Emily on the blue velvet seat, with Dinah opposite, she saw him solicitously urge his wife into the inn, out of the chilly wind. Charlotte turned on the doorstep for one last wave as the carriage jolted into motion.

Was she really Giles's great-grandmother? Jodie wondered. If the twentieth-century Lady Faringdale had a family tree or a copy of Burke's Peerage, she could look it up. But a family tree might show that Charlotte had died in childbirth. Jodie decided that she couldn't bear to find out, even if they arrived home safely, and if Giles did not immediately bundle his discreditable charge back to her digs in Oxford.

Despite the dank weather, Giles had chosen to ride. In

her misery, Jodie was unable to take any pleasure in the greening hedgerows. They were moving slowly enough to see a few primroses raising their pale faces above rosettes of crinkled leaves, vivid clusters of violets nodding in the breeze—slowly, that is, compared to a car. By contemporary standards they raced along, Lord Thorncrest driving as if they really had to reach Bristol.

In Coventry, however, he handed the reins to his coachman and joined Giles on horseback. After stopping for luncheon at the Swan in Banbury, they reached Waterstock in mid afternoon.

Harry Font's preparations were well under way. Behind the stables, several planks raised on bricks bore a row of large glass jars lined with foil and linked by pink-gleaming copper wire. From the end of the row a wire stretched up to the tile roof, where it coiled around one of the lightning rods.

Leaving the gentlemen fussing over what Harry called a Voltaic Cell and Giles called a battery, Jodie and Emily went into the house. Mrs. Briggs greeted them with a tea tray, not at all put out by their unexpected arrival.

A groom had carried their portmanteaux up to their chambers and when they went up Dinah had already unpacked. She had left Jodie's few twentieth-century belongings on top of the dresser.

"Reckon you'll be wanting to take them home with you, miss," she explained.

There was the book that had caused so much trouble, the tote-bag, the bra and pantyhose she had been reduced to in the stables that stormy night. . . .

"I can't go back in my underwear!" she exclaimed in horror.

Emily giggled. "How you shocked me that night. Of course not, you shall wear one of my gowns."

"Can you spare the one you were wearing when we arrived? The green jumper—pinafore dress? Otherwise I'm going to have some explaining to do when it disappears and another turns up in its place. Oh lord, I've just thought—it's all very well taking all my notes home and using them for my thesis, but if anyone asks my sources I'll be stumped."

"Sources?" Emily looked puzzled.

Jodie explained the need for documentation. "If they test the paper and ink," she went on, "they'll be the right type but they'll seem brand new. It'll look like a forgery."

"Hide them. Let us tuck them away somewhere where no one will find them, then you can fetch them out and they will be as old as they should be."

"Genius!" Jodie hugged her. "I only hope Charles appreciates what he's getting. Where do you suggest?"

"The attics, I should think, though we had best ask Giles where they are least likely to be disturbed."

As far as Giles knew, the attics would remain unaltered, unvisited except for repairs to the roof and the addition of more junk to that already accumulated. Jodie's notes, in a metal box to keep out mice, were duly stowed in a distant corner behind a loose board. Jodie and Emily climbed down the stepladder with cobwebs in their hair, to find that Mrs. Briggs had had the boiler heated for the shower-bath.

The conversation at dinner was monopolized by Giles and Harry discussing incomprehensible numbers. Afterwards the two scientists disappeared into the library to do some final figuring.

In the drawing room, Emily sat down to play the pianoforte, and Thorncrest hovered over her with a besotted air. Though Jodie was glad to see his growing affection, she felt excluded, set at a distance by both their closeness and her own coming departure. She shivered. This time tomorrow, would the atoms of her body be scattered across a thousand galaxies? Would her mind confront the incomprehensible realities of a strange dimension?

Perhaps she should stay after all?

Harry put the question to her at breakfast the next morning. "I know Giles told you of the danger," he said quietly. "I want you to know that if you decide to stay, Cassandra and I will always be happy to offer you a home."

Jodie had to decide. She looked around the table. There was Emily, her dear face sweet and solemn in the pale light of daybreak; Charles Thorncrest, who had turned out to be a pretty cool guy after all; Harry—he and Cassandra would welcome her. She thought of Charlotte and Roland, of the loving couple she had watched them becoming. She thought of living through the history she had studied, being a part of it. . . .

And there was Giles, curiously out of place in his grey track suit, intent on Emily's soft words. Though he had scarcely spoken to Jodie since persuading her to give up the abduction, she could not give up hope of regaining his regard. And even if that proved impossible, like him she had too much calling her home.

If she ceased to exist, she would never know it. If by some chance she and Giles emerged in another time and place, at least he would be with her. He would never abandon her. Together they would go adventuring again; one way or another she would win his love. In the end, if he was there what did it matter where she found herself?

"No," she said to Harry. "Thank you, but I'm going."

He pulled out his watch. "Then it's time we were moving."

In case of an accident, all the horses had been taken out to pasture. The stables were gloomy and silent without their usual inhabitants. Jodie had grown used to the all-pervasive smell of horses in this society and scarcely noticed it as, final farewells over, she and Giles took their places in the stall where they had arrived.

They stood close to the back wall where the lightning conductors merged before grounding. Harry was outside by the battery with his chronometer, ready to touch wire to wire at the precisely calculated moment. Emily and Thorncrest stood by the stable door, silhouetted against the grey daylight.

Jodie felt sick. "I'm scared to death," she whispered to Giles.

He took her in his arms and bent his head to kiss her.

"The devil!" Thorncrest exclaimed. "If that's what morals will come to . . ."

Emily interrupted. "Did we never tell you they are not really brother and sister? They are not even related."

"In that case," said the earl promptly, "I consider that they are setting us an excellent example."

Over Giles's shoulder, Jodie saw him pull Emily into a

passionate embrace. Giles's mouth was soft and warm on hers; she closed her eyes, giving herself up to the sensations that raced through her. There was a thunderous *crack* . . .

. . . and October sunshine poured through the wide windows, gleaming on machined metal. A faint hum filled the air, air that was strangely flat without the smell of horses.

Giles pulled away from her, the startled look in his blue eyes reflecting her own disorientation. He ran his fingers through his hair.

"It wasn't a dream, was it?" he asked uncertainly. "Have I really been kissing you for nearly two centuries?"

"It didn't feel that long."

"Oh. Then I'd better do it again."

Jodie was not about to protest. This time their kiss lasted mere minutes, yet this time Jodie was left breathless.

Was it possible he didn't despise her after all? She didn't dare ask.

"It wasn't a dream, was it?" she repeated his words in a dazed voice. "Two hundred years—we can't have dreamed the same dream."

At once he became practical. "Let's go and look for your papers in the attic."

Jodie wondered what he was feeling as they crossed the courtyard and went into the house. To him, all this had been familiar all his life. To her, more familiar with Water- stock Manor as it had been two hundred years ago, every- thing was slightly wrong. She was constantly on the verge of *déjà vu*, a most unsettling sensation.

She concentrated on the lithe figure leading the way up the stairs—only to find that sight more unsettling still.

Had he forgiven her for her idiotic project?

The attic was dim and dusty, more cluttered than she remembered it. They crouched together under the rafters in the corner. She pulled out the loose board and there was the tin chest, just where she and Emily had put it last night.

Emily! A pang of sorrow shook Jodie. Emily was long dead. The kiss she had shared with Charles Thorncrest in the stables that grey spring day had long since lost its meaning.

"Shall I open it?" Giles took the box from her memory-stilled hands. "The hinges are a bit rusty. There we are."

On top of the roll of papers lay three loose sheets, yellow with age, the writing faded. Jodie picked them up with utmost care and hunched backwards to inspect them in the light from a roof vent.

"From Emily! Oh Giles, she wrote this when she was seventy! Charles has just died—I don't want to think about that yet." She put the page behind the others. Giles crouched next to her, his arm about her waist, reading over her shoulder. "What's this one? Ah, that's better. She's twenty-five, she and Charles have travelled a great deal but now they are settling down because she is pregnant. And there's a postscript, six years later. She had a daughter and they christened her Jodie." Her voice caught in her throat. "She never forgot us."

"The last line is best: Charles spoils them both to death. What's the last paper?"

"A family tree. It's in Emily's writing but the names at the top are Roland and Charlotte! Charlotte's pregnancy went okay then. Thank heaven. And look! They called their daughter Judith and their son Giles."

Giles grinned hugely. "I wager I'm the only person who's ever had an ancestor named after him!"

"So we started your family tradition. How strange!" Jodie looked at the next page, but it was the one written when Emily was seventy. She wasn't ready to read it. "That's all, nothing from Charlotte. She wouldn't forget us either, but I expect within a month or two she persuaded herself that we really went back to America. I'm going to miss them all horribly."

"I was afraid for a while that you were going to stay," said Giles sombrely. "You were so mad at me for stopping you from saving Ada."

"Mad at you? No I wasn't." She concentrated on putting the papers carefully back in the box.

"Then why were you so silent? Why did you avoid me?"

"I was sure you despised me for trying that wicked scheme to kidnap Ada Byron."

"Not wicked, love, just unwise. How could I despise you when your only thought was for her welfare?"

"You said you were going home and gave me a choice whether to go too. I thought you'd be glad to get rid of me."

"I couldn't have left without you."

"You couldn't?" She twisted her neck to look up at him. "What did you call me just now?"

"Love."

"The English call everyone love."

"I don't. Jodie, I . . . ." He was interrupted by the boom of a gong, reverberating through the floorboards. "Damn. That means tea's ready. Well it can wait, we just ate breakfast."

Afraid that he was not going to say what she wanted him to say, she scrambled to get out of their corner. "Oh no, it would be shockingly uncivil to keep your mother waiting. Ouch!" She knocked her head on a beam, dislodging the elegant Regency hairstyle. "Come on. I'll go down the ladder first and you hand me the box. I'll put it in my bedchamber—oh, I don't have a bedchamber here. Drat, I can see this is going to be excessively confusing."

"I'm pretty confused myself," said Giles, following her, "but if you want a bedchamber I'll be happy to oblige."

Jodie decided to ignore the implications of that remark for the moment. They left the box on a hall table and she hurried him down the stairs. Suddenly it was very important not to offend Lady Faringdale.

The sitting room was as comfortable as ever it had been in the days when it was known as the morning parlour. The viscountess, though nothing like Charlotte in appearance, was equally welcoming. The tanned, lined face of the perpetual English gardener bore an expression that at once reminded Jodie of the glint of amusement that so often lurked in the depths of Giles's blue eyes.

"Mother, this is Jodie Far . . . Zaleski. She's a Rhodes scholar from California."

Jodie curtsied—and flushed in embarrassment. Both the curtsy and the blush were habits she would have to unlearn.

"How do you do," said Lady Faringdale. "So Giles talked

you into trying on that old dress. You look very nice in it, my dear, but what were you thinking of, Giles, to drag the poor girl backwards through a haystack?"

Giles looked at her and grinned. "She is a bit dishevelled, isn't she? I hadn't noticed. Oh, hold still a minute, Jodie, there's a spider in your hair." He removed the offending arachnid, together with a good part of its web, and deposited them in a nearby wastepaper basket.

Jodie's face burned. With her eyes fixed on the spider as it climbed out and spun down to the carpet, she said, "I'm so sorry, my lady. I should have tidied myself." And she had hoped to make a good impression!

"Rubbish, it was entirely Giles's fault for not telling you the haystack had pulled you about."

"Not a haystack, Mother; we were in the attics. The gong interrupted a proposal."

"In the attics! How odd you young people are. Of course, that's exactly what my parents used to say, but I don't remember ever being proposed to in an attic. Do sit down, Jodie. What did you answer?"

Jodie's head whirled as Giles drew her close.

"I didn't actually manage to pop the question."

"Then do get it over with, dear, while I pour the tea. Do you take milk and sugar, Jodie?"

Jodie's knees were weak. She sank onto the nearest sofa. "Black, thank you, my lady. Do you mean it, Giles?"

In approved Regency style, he dropped to one sweatsuited knee before her. "It is the dearest wish of my heart, love. Though we met this morning, I have adored you for centuries. Will you do me the honour of becoming my wife?"

Looking into his sky-blue eyes Jodie saw there the respect and passion and tenderness that added up to his love for her. She reached out and pressed the back of her hand to his cheek. He caught it and kissed it.

"Oh Giles, yes please. I've loved you for centuries too."

"Very nice, my dears," said Lady Faringdale, and passed the tea.

If you would like to receive details of other Walker Regency Romances, please write to:

Regency Editor
Walker and Company
720 Fifth Avenue
New York, NY 10019